IN THEIR HANDS
THEIR CAPTIVE BRIDE #1

JULIA SYKES

Copyright © 2022 by Julia Sykes

All rights reserved.

No part of this book may be reproduced in any form or by any electronic or mechanical means, including information storage and retrieval systems, without written permission from the author, except for the use of brief quotations in a book review.

Cover image: Wander Aguiar

Cover Design: PopKitty Design

Editing: Rebecca Cartee, Editing by Rebecca

CHAPTER 1
NORA

"Hello, little bird." A deep voice skated over the back of my neck like velvet, making my nerves jump. "I've been waiting for you."

I whirled, heart jumping into my throat at the man's proximity. In a hurry to obey my father's demand for a meeting in his study, I hadn't noticed the stranger lurking in the shadows of our cavernous foyer. He leaned casually against the banister of the curved double staircase, head tipped at a curious angle. Vibrant green eyes clashed with my shocked hazel gaze, his glittering with amusement that held an arrogant edge. His square jaw was darkened by stubble, which matched the slightly untidy tumble of dark curls around his angelically perfect face.

A fallen angel, judging by the way he was looking at me. His eyes roved over each of my facial features before dipping lower for a fraction of a heartbeat: a brief but intimate appraisal. His white teeth flashed in a purely predatory smile, and he prowled toward me. As he stepped fully into the light, the shadows cleared from beneath his high cheekbones, and recognition finally dawned.

Dante Torrio. I'd seen him at my father's parties, but I didn't truly know him. He was too painfully beautiful to look straight at him, like staring into the sun. And Father never allowed us to interact with men beyond a polite smile and demure nod.

He reached the edge of my personal space, then stepped into it as though he had every right. He towered over me, almost a foot taller than my five-foot five frame. Those striking eyes pinned me in place, peering straight into me. The slightly cruel twist of his full lips sliced into my chest, stealing my breath. His sudden nearness was shocking, his masculine scent suffusing the air around me with a foreign, enticing perfume. I'd never stood so close to a man; men were forbidden. Well, the only time I was this close was when Father tasked one of his goons with punishing me.

But this was different. Dante wasn't looking at me with malice in his glittering eyes. The sharpness that pierced my soul was something hungrier than violence. My belly flipped, and I took a wary step back.

His grin turned lopsided, amused by my trepidation. A shiver raced down my spine, and warmth suffused my cheeks.

I took another step back, licking my suddenly dry lips. Dante's gaze darkened as he watched the flick of my tongue and focused on my mouth. Something clenched between my legs, and my face burned with an embarrassed flush. His intense attention made me squirm, and judging by the perverse pleasure that illuminated his sharp features, he was enjoying my apprehension.

I lifted my chin and met his taunting gaze head-on. All my life, my will had been crushed by brutal men, any signs of defiance quickly obliterated by a harsh slap or thundering shout. But no matter how many times I had to swallow my pride and bend, I kept my righteous rage stoked deep inside my chest.

Dante wasn't one of my father's men. He had no right to punish me. And I didn't have to stand in his imposing shadow, shrinking beneath his cocky, self-assured stare.

His smile sharpened to something almost feral, and he grasped my hand with thick fingers, drawing my arm through his with a gentle but unbreakable grip. Sparks tingled where our skin touched, his rough callouses rasping over my softer palm. He rested my hand on his forearm, and I felt the raw power of his corded muscles even through his perfectly tailored suit.

Something tugged at the pit of my stomach, as though pulling me closer to his heat, his intoxicating scent.

I swallowed hard. "I have to go." I hated the way my voice wavered, and I didn't pull away from his allure.

I had to go meet my father in his study, or I would definitely be punished for my tardiness. No matter how fascinating I found this unnerving connection to Dante, it was dangerous. In so many ways. If Father saw me touching him...

I tried to yank my hand free, but his fingers firmed around mine, gluing my palm to his arm.

He started walking with sure, confident strides, as though he was escorting me to a ball.

"We're going to the same place," he informed me, his voice still lilting with amusement. He liked that he was making me hot and flustered.

Defiant anger spiked, cracking my usual composure. I jerked away from him. "Let me go!"

I stumbled as he abruptly released me. His mocking chuckle rolled over my skin, making my flesh pebble and dance as though at a physical touch.

My cheeks burned with anger and embarrassment, and I quickly righted myself. I walked stiffly toward my father's study, my low, sensible heels clicking across the marble foyer. Dante kept step beside me, half an inch too close for polite company. I could still smell his heady cologne, and his body heat caressed my side. His dark pleasure and masculine power pulsed over me, and I suppressed the tremor that teased along my bones.

I wouldn't show further weakness. And I wouldn't let him touch me again. Not when I knew he wouldn't be the one to suffer the consequences; Father would have a fit if he knew I'd allowed a man to touch me.

I took a breath and settled my features into the composed expression that was my best protection against men's cruel interest. If I gave them no reason to be angry with me, I wouldn't be hurt. The small, serene smile was a mask that shielded the fire in my soul. They wouldn't try to snuff it out if I didn't let them see it.

Despite my calm demeanor, familiar dread weighed in my stomach, growing heavier with each step toward the study. Nothing good ever happened to me in that room. I was either called in for a reprimand or unpleasant news. My fingers flexed at my sides in a fruitless attempt to release some of the mounting anxiety that wound my muscles tighter with each passing second.

"Do I make you nervous, little bird?" That mocking, amused tone again, but slightly deeper this time, another velvet caress.

I'd almost forgotten about Dante's imposing presence at my side as my worry escalated, and I jolted slightly at his question.

"You're not the one I'm worried about," I answered honestly before I could think better of telling the truth.

I didn't know Dante at all, and showing any man a shred of vulnerability usually ended in more pain. Father's men liked inflicting pain. He selected them as his guards for their sadistic tendencies; he liked to inspire fear.

I edged away from Dante. I'd heard stories about his sadistic nature too. The urbane man strolling casually at my side was capable of shocking, brutal violence that made even the hardest men in our organization tread lightly in his presence.

He made a low humming sound that was almost a growl. It rumbled along my bones, drawing another shiver to the surface of my skin.

Too soon, we reached the threshold to the study. Instinct made me want to draw in a deep breath to fortify myself, but I didn't dare. I arranged my face in a careful, pleasant mask and lifted my chin as I stepped inside.

Father sat behind his enormous, imposing mahogany desk, flanked by Giorgio, his most vicious bodyguard. My father was still fearsome and ruthless, but age stooped his shoulders, and the beginnings of arthritis curled his fingers. He wasn't physically capable of doling out the violence he'd once been renowned for. There was a reason he'd earned his place as consigliere of the

Vitale crime family, Tommaso Vitale's right-hand man.

Tommaso, the boss of the organization, was in even poorer health than my father, on his deathbed if the rumors were to be believed. Heart disease didn't discriminate. It would take down the terrifying crime boss more cruelly than any bullet he'd dodged over the years.

I ignored the sharp glint in my father's hazel eyes and went to join my sister, Giana. Her olive toned features were nearly identical to mine, but her trepidation made her appear slighter than me, younger despite the fact that she'd been born eighteen months earlier. The glimmers of golden strands shone through her brown hair, making her appear like a delicate, ethereal nymph in the low lighting of the opulent study.

Wood paneled walls surrounded us, closing in tighter with each of my carefully measured breaths. I wanted to take Giana's hand in mine and give it a reassuring squeeze, but I knew Giorgio's black eyes would immediately take note of the small show of weakness. Giana was fragile enough as it was, almost trembling in the burly guard's shadow; she didn't need any sign of comfort from me to signal further vulnerability.

"Dante, thank you for coming," Father greeted as the impossibly handsome, disconcerting man entered the study behind me. I felt his heat at my back, still a little too close for polite company.

I released a small breath when he strolled past me, and the sense that I was being watched like prey finally eased. His focus was on my father now, and I nearly sagged with relief; I hadn't realized how his attention had put all my survival instincts on high alert, and now that his intense gaze shifted, I felt almost lightheaded at the release.

Dante tipped his head in an almost imperceptible nod, the barest show of submission. "I'm always happy to accept an invitation from you, Giuseppe."

My father leaned forward on his elbows, his sharp gaze skewering the younger man. Dante didn't so much as flinch. He met Father's bone-quaking stare head on.

"Tommaso is dying," Father said bluntly, cutting right to the chase with his usual battering ram approach to negotiations. "As you know, he expects his son, Luca, to take his place at the head of our family."

The barest hint of a shadow flickered across

Dante's stubble-shaded jaw, so fast I might have imagined it.

"You know why you're here," Father continued. "Luca isn't strong enough to hold off the Russians when they come circling in the wake of Tommaso's death."

"Agreed," Dante replied coolly, dark brows lowering slightly over his keen eyes.

"And that little shit will get rid of me as soon as he can manage to stick a knife in my back."

I jolted at that revelation. I was mostly kept apart from family politics. I knew my father was as close as a brother to Tommaso, but I'd had no idea that Tommaso's son would turn on him at the first opportunity. What had Father done to incite Luca's ire?

"You want an alliance," Dante said it like it was a foregone conclusion, a fact that had been established before we'd stepped into this meeting.

Father tipped his head in acknowledgement, but the direction of his gaze flicked to Giana and me. I stiffened, unease coiling in the pit of my stomach. Why were we here? There was no reason for my sister and me to silently witness this meeting; we certainly hadn't been called here to offer our opinions or input.

"I'm backing you," Father announced, his attention spearing Dante once again. "I will keep my position. I will be your consigliere, and you will take control of the organization. I'm too old to be the boss. My health is already failing. You're strong enough to push back the Bratva and even take more territory from them. You have the instincts and temperament for the job. You came up from nothing, and you're our most powerful capo now. I choose you to be Tommaso's successor, even if he thinks his son should come to power after his death." His eyes lifted in a brief prayer, as though asking for forgiveness for betraying his closest friend's wishes.

I continued to watch the exchange in tense silence, my mind racing. Giana and I shouldn't be here. We shouldn't know about Father's planned coup. It put us in danger, and for all my father's cruelty, he'd always protected us from the worst aspects of his criminal lifestyle. The violence we suffered at home was nothing compared to his vicious capabilities when it came to his enemies.

Or, it seemed, his supposed allies. He was prepared to turn on Luca and upend the organization's power structure in order to cling to his position as consigliere.

Dante's vibrant eyes cut into me before flicking back to my father. "And how do you propose we seal this alliance?" Again, that almost bored tone, as though he'd known exactly how this conversation would go before he'd even arrived at my house.

Father's edict dropped like a stone between us: "You will marry my eldest daughter, Giana."

My sister's sharp gasp spiked through my heart, her fear lancing me with rage. My fingers curled at my sides, and my spine stiffened. She might be the eldest, but I'd always been her protector. She trembled at my side, wilting at the prospect of my father's command.

I stepped in front of her, shielding her from him and from Dante's arrogant gaze. How dare they treat my sister like an object to be traded? She was kind and gentle, and she deserved to be loved, not used like a pawn in a mobster's power play.

"I won't let you do this," I seethed, my defiant stare clashing with Dante's intense green eyes. They flared slightly, darkening with some emotion I didn't fully understand.

I ignored the strange look and took a step toward him, getting in his personal space as though I could physically intimidate the mountain of a man. "I won't let you anywhere near my sister."

The capo was a monster with a fearsome reputation. He would be cold and possibly abusive to Giana, and she was far too frail to withstand that kind of cruelty. She would wither and waste away if I allowed them to cage her in an arranged marriage with a heartless bastard.

Dante had unnerved me during our brief exchange in the foyer; Giana would crumble if he turned that intense attention on her.

I dared to take my eyes off the threat so that I could glare at my father. "You can't sell Giana like this. I won't allow it. If Mom were here—"

"Don't talk to me about your mother!" Father boomed. "I won't tolerate this disrespect."

He nodded at Giorgio, and suddenly the beast was looming over me. Pain cracked through my skull when his meaty hand collided with my cheek. I reeled, black flickering over my vision as a hundred bees stung my face. My eyes watered, blurring the room. Giana's arms were around me, holding me upright when the world tilted.

In the heartbeat of dizziness, a terrible snarl ripped through the study, followed by a booming thud. I blinked hard, desperate to assess my surroundings and avoid the worst of the next blow.

But the hit didn't come. Through my watery vision, I saw Dante holding Giorgio up by his neck as though he weighed nothing, pinning him against the bookcase with one huge hand wrapped around the guard's throat. Shock punched me at the sudden violence, taking my breath away. Dante's beautiful features were twisted into something almost feral.

"Dante!" Father barked, a thread of fear in his voice.

The younger man didn't heed the warning. His full lips peeled back from his teeth as he lowered his face closer to Giorgio's purple features.

"No one touches what's mine," he snarled at the man who'd been my tormentor for years.

My stomach dropped to the floor, and my head spun. I couldn't fully take in the implications of his furious words.

"That's enough," Father insisted, the command hitching slightly.

"Apologize," Dante hissed in Giorgio's rapidly darkening face. My assailant twisted and struggled for air.

"I'm...sorry," he gasped out when Dante loosened his grip a fraction to allow him space to suck in a tiny breath.

"Don't look at me when you say it," Dante said, his voice going cold and more tightly controlled, some of the primal ferocity ebbing away. "Look at her."

Giorgio's eyes rolled with fear, but he managed to direct them at me. "I'm sorry," he forced out, tears streaming down his face.

Dante dropped him like garbage, stepped away, and straightened his suit. The snarl had melted, and he was coolly composed once again, as though he hadn't just nearly strangled a man to death.

"I accept your alliance," he told my father. "But I'm marrying Elenora, not Giana."

As my mind spun, Father's eyes narrowed, bristling at the challenge. "She's my youngest. Giana should be married first."

Dante met him head-on. "It's Elenora, or the deal is off. She will be my wife, or I walk away right now."

"You wouldn't dare," Father shot back. "You want this too badly. You've been working toward it your entire life."

Dante's head tipped back, his lip curling with

contempt. "I can take control without your help, old man. I'm offering you a seat at the table. All I ask in exchange is your daughter, a price you were already willing to pay."

My fingernails cut into my palms, and I bit the inside of my cheek as I trapped defiant words behind my pursed lips. I wanted to rail at him that I wasn't an object to be traded any more than my sister was. But I could see the cold determination in Dante's glittering eyes. He would take what he wanted, one way or another. He would step over my father's dead body to seize control of the organization. And then, he could claim anything he desired. Including my sister.

I wouldn't let him have her. This monster of a man wouldn't touch Giana. For some reason, he preferred me at the moment, and I wouldn't give him a chance to change his mind.

"I'll do it," I forced out through gritted teeth.

"Nora, no!" Giana exclaimed, her hand suddenly a vise around my clenched fist.

I shook her off and squared my shoulders, facing Dante with defiance and determination. If this beast of a man was going to marry one of us, it would be me.

Sparks danced in the depths of his deep green

eyes, and his lips curled at the corners, that amused expression once again gracing his painfully handsome face. I suppressed a shudder and kept him locked in my stare.

"I will marry you," I said, the oath ashes on my tongue.

The words were surreal, as though they were issued from someone else's lips. But Dante's intense gaze kept me riveted, rooted in this awful reality so that I felt every aching beat of my racing heart as it hammered against my ribs.

Two thick fingers curled beneath my chin, gently turning my face so that he could inspect my stinging cheek. His dark brows drew low over his eyes, and angry lines appeared around his mouth.

"No one else will touch you ever again, little bird," he promised, his voice a low rumble. He spoke as though it was a reassurance, not a horrific claim over my future, my forever.

"Girls, leave us," Father snapped. "Dante and I have a lot to discuss."

Giana's small hand wrapped around mine, tugging me away from the predator who held my chin with such shocking gentleness. He'd just strangled Giorgio with the same long fingers that now caressed my face.

My breath stuttered, and I allowed Giana to pull me away from the man who'd just condemned me to a life sentence. My *fiancé*. I would marry this brute. I would've done anything to protect my beloved sister, but my insides began to quake at the reality of the commitment I'd just made.

In the back of my mind, I'd always known such an arranged marriage was a possibility. In our world, a love match was too much to hope for. Especially if my father was the one making the arrangements. He'd never miss an opportunity to secure more power, and if that meant using his own daughters to solidify an alliance, he wouldn't hesitate.

But that was always a vague future prospect that I hadn't allowed myself to fully contemplate. I'd allowed my head to fill with fantasies of romance based on the novels I indulged in secret. I'd hoped that my father's emotional neglect might extend to my future prospects and that he wouldn't care about my marital preferences. I would never be allowed a match with someone outside our organization, but I might've chosen someone gentler than Dante Torrio.

If his scheme with my father worked, Dante

would be the boss. He would rule our crime family with an iron fist, and that would include me.

He'd just committed shocking violence to claim me for himself.

No one else will touch you ever again, little bird. From now on, Dante would personally be the one to keep me in line. I no longer had to fear my father's men, but my future husband was far more terrifying than even Giorgio, his cruelest guard.

My fingers went numb in Giana's as she urged me out of the study and back into the hall. My chest grew tighter with every quick step across the burgundy rug.

"I'll get you out of this, Nora," she pledged shakily. "I won't let this happen."

"No," I refused, my tongue feeling strangely thick in my mouth. "He can't have you. I can handle him."

She clutched my hand more tightly. "I won't let you do this for me." Her voice wavered with tears. "He's a monster, Nora. You can't marry him."

My lungs seized. I couldn't draw in enough air to argue with her. I rushed toward the front door, bursting out into the crisp fall air. It seared my lungs as I gasped in deep gulps of fresh oxygen.

Dizziness swept over me, and I didn't see the

men coming for us until it was too late. Tires screeched as brakes slammed, and the doors on three black SUVs flew open. A dozen men surged toward us, and Giana's scream ripped into my chest. The fearful sound sharpened my senses, adrenaline spiking to throw everything into sharp relief. Time slowed, and I saw the huge man who made a grab for her: Luca Vitale. I'd memorized his strong, stony features over the years, harboring a foolish crush on the ruggedly handsome man.

There was nothing charming about his ochre eyes now. They were dark with grim determination as his meaty hand closed around Giana's arm.

"You saved me the trouble of coming in to get you," he rumbled, tugging her close.

I threw myself at him, shoving at his brick-hard chest. "Let her go!"

He sneered at me, unmoving under my assault. "I'm here for Dante's bride. Your father is a traitor. He'll pay for that. Now, get out of my way."

My heart leapt into my throat, but I managed to force words past it. "She's not his bride. I am."

His brows drew together, and he paused his progress in dragging Giana back to the SUV. "But you're Elenora."

"Yes," I seethed, hating him with every fiber of

my being. Hating Dante. Hating my father. "I'm Elenora, and I'm supposed to marry that monster, not Giana."

I couldn't let Luca take her away from here. He'd clearly learned of my father's betrayal somehow, and he'd come to destroy those plans by stealing Dante's bride away. We truly were nothing more than pawns to these awful men.

"If you're looking for Dante's fiancée, I'm right here," I flung at him, shoving his chest once again. He didn't so much as sway beneath the impact.

His lips pressed together in a grim line, and he released Giana. I didn't have time to draw in a relieved breath before his hands closed around my waist. The world spun, and my abdomen collided with his muscular shoulder. I shrieked and struggled as he carried me away from my sister.

She screamed my name as Luca hauled me toward the waiting SUV, stealing me from Dante as though I was his property, his prize of war.

My fists beat against Luca's back, my body refusing to simply surrender to this awful fate. His thick fingers dug into my upper thigh, just beneath my bottom. I cursed him and twisted, unable to shift so much as an inch out of his hold.

Then I was in the car, his strong arms caging

me as the door slammed shut like a prison cell. We peeled away from the curb, leaving my sister screaming on the pavement outside our family home.

I looked up into my captor's light brown eyes, finding no warmth in their caramel depths.

"Where are you taking me?" I demanded, voice shaking almost as violently as my hands.

"To get married," he said coldly. "You're not Dante's bride. You're mine."

CHAPTER 2
NORA

"This is insane," I said before I could think better of it, the accusation breathless and a little too high-pitched. "You can't just steal me away like I'm an object. I don't want to marry you."

Luca's eyes darkened. "And you prefer Dante as your husband? The man is a sadist."

I shuddered at the warning in his tone, but I couldn't stop protesting. The shock of being kidnapped and told I would be forced into marriage was too terrifying to suppress my emotions like I usually did. "I don't want to marry anyone!"

His square jaw firmed to a grim line. "I hadn't planned on marriage today either, but sometimes we don't get a choice. Dante can't have you. I won't let him take what's mine."

"I'm not yours!"

"I'm talking about my birthright," he snapped. "But yes, Elenora. You'll be mine within the hour. It's done. Don't be difficult."

I stiffened. "And what are you going to do? Beat me if I don't agree to walk down the aisle?"

He was suddenly in my personal space, looming over me. The air in the car turned thick, too heavy to breathe. There was only his menacing power pulsing over me, emanating from his huge frame to suffocate me. His big arms caged me, one hand pressed against the seat and the other on the window beside my head.

"Listen to me, Elenora. I have no intention of abusing you. But you will be an obedient wife."

Fear raced down my spine, but I tipped my chin back, defiant. "I won't. I won't marry you."

Dark brows drew together. "Do you have any idea what Dante does to women? If you were his, he would hurt you, and he would enjoy it."

I thought of Dante's twisted snarl as he'd strangled Giorgio, the violence that'd rippled through his muscular body. I didn't manage to suppress a shiver.

Luca's lips twisted with distaste. "That's your alternative. If you cooperate, you have nothing to fear from me."

"Why do you even want to marry me?" I challenged, desperation bleeding through my anger. Luca had never paid any attention to me before, even though I'd harbored a crush on the ruggedly handsome man.

That crush seemed ludicrous now. All I wanted was to escape from his overbearing aura and insane demands.

Being sold into an arranged marriage had been terrifying enough; Luca had kidnapped me and was telling me that I'd be forced to marry him against my will. Dante scared me, but in this moment, Luca was the more terrifying monster.

He grimaced. "I won't start a war within our own organization. I don't intend to tear the family apart before I even take control. Your father has made an error in judgment. Not all of his men agree with his scheme to choose Dante over me. They came to me and told me about his plans. I won't kill your father because too many of our men respect him. I might hate the old bastard, but I won't spill his blood. But the alliance with Dante won't go forward. I'll have his daughter under my control, and your father will fall in line."

"So, I'm your hostage, then," I said bitterly.

"You'll be my wife," he bit out. "It doesn't have to be unpleasant for you. I take care of my own."

"I'm not yours," I insisted again. "I'll never be yours. I don't belong to anyone but myself."

A shadow danced over his granite jaw. "You're wrong, Elenora. You belong to me now. Whether you like it or not is your choice."

With each damning statement, he leaned closer, his quick breaths hot on my cheeks.

I suppressed a shiver and gathered my courage. "I won't marry you."

His lips pressed to a grim line, holding in further words of rebuke. For a tense moment, I thought I might've held my ground. I thought he would let me go.

My heart leapt into my throat when his big hands bracketed my waist, dragging me toward him. I released a harsh cry as he manhandled me, fear searing through my righteous fury. I struggled, limbs swinging wildly. My fist glanced off his jaw, and he growled in warning. His hands clamped my wrists, pulling my arms behind my back and pinning them there. He used the leverage to shove me down, until I was draped over his lap. I writhed, shrieking in animal panic and rage as the world swirled around me. I couldn't think; all that existed was deep, primal fear that coursed through my veins with every rapid beat of my heart.

One of his huge hands easily shackled my wrists, and the other gripped the hem of my skirt. He yanked the material up, and I choked on a shocked cry as he stripped away my modesty, leaving my white cotton underwear exposed. Leaving *me* exposed. I suddenly felt small and unbearably vulnerable.

My scream died in my throat. "What are you doing?" I managed to force myself to form a coherent question, but it was little more than a breathless whisper. There wasn't enough oxygen in the car.

"You will be my wife, Elenora." His dark warning was followed by a sharp slap, and a rush of heat stung my bottom. Before I could draw in the air to cry out, he landed another blow. "You will obey me." Another slap, another gasp for breath. "You will not fight me on this."

"Stop!" I managed to beg. My soul was laid

bare, my will stripped away even more ruthlessly than he'd yanked away my modesty.

"I'll stop when you agree to behave." His voice had deepened. He sounded calmer, sterner. There was no hint of a growl in his words this time. He'd fully subjugated me, and he had his more volatile emotions back under control.

I knew monsters like him: men who got off on holding power over weaker women.

"You're a brute," I hissed, hating him with every fiber of my being.

Three more stinging swats, and my bottom was on fire. I howled and kicked out, my heels banging against the car door. He didn't relent. Heat flared beneath his calloused palm, thrumming deep into my flesh. It made something ache deep inside me, a strange throb that echoed each slap.

My cry morphed into a mortified gasp. Some part of my mind registered what that feeling was: arousal. My panties grew damp, and my cheeks burned more hotly than my skin beneath his punitive hand.

This couldn't be happening. My stupid crush on Luca had clearly scrambled my brain, making me react to his touch. It hurt. And it felt good in the most forbidden, cruel way.

The hits stopped, and he rubbed his palm over my enflamed flesh. A sound like a humiliating whimper eased from my throat, and I pressed my face into the seat as though I could hide from him. The scent of leather flooded my senses, but it didn't quite drown out the smell of my traitorous arousal in the tight space of the car.

Oh, god. We weren't alone in here. There were two men in the front seats. They might not be looking at me, but they'd witnessed the mortifying scene; they'd heard Luca disciplining me like a child.

Thick fingers skimmed over my stinging skin, and the gentle sensation was almost unbearably decadent after the pain of the spanking. I bit my lip against a groan of relief and turned my cheek farther into the seat, wishing I could melt away into nothing.

"We could get along, Elenora." This time, there was a deep rumble of satisfaction in Luca's voice.

His fingers dipped between my legs, the barest brush against my wet underwear. I couldn't help myself; I bucked against his hand, too shocked and confused to control my body. He'd taken control of my entire being, and I felt like I was spiraling into a black abyss. I clung on to sanity by a thread.

"Please," I begged. "Stop."

"Are you going to behave?" he asked, voice deep and dark with warning.

"Yes," I squeaked, swallowing a sob. I wouldn't cry. Not for him. If I stopped resisting, he couldn't break me completely. I would comply with his insane demands. It was the only way I could survive this day with some of my dignity intact.

Drawing on years of practice, I shoved my emotions down deep, crushing my pain, humiliation, and fury into a tight little ball and burying it in the pit of my stomach. I drew in a deep breath and softened in his unyielding hold.

I would endure. I would not let a man break me. I would comply, but I wouldn't allow him to reduce me to a shell of myself.

Luca's touch was almost tender as he slowly tugged my skirt back down over my thighs, his fingertips trailing along my sensitized skin. He released my wrists and grasped my waist, carefully guiding me to sit beside him. Heated pain flared on my abused bottom, and I suppressed a grimace, struggling to keep my face calm and composed. I wouldn't let him see how thoroughly he'd rattled me.

He rested his hand on my knee, maintaining contact. Despite my desire to escape him entirely, the temptation to find comfort in that simple touch was nearly overwhelming. My eyes burned, and I blinked rapidly to clear the haze of tears before they could fall down my cheeks.

I stared out the car window, hiding my eyes from him so that he couldn't see them shining. The world blurred past us, the result of my disorientation rather than the speed of the SUV. We'd slowed to follow normal traffic laws; Luca wouldn't want to be pulled over and questioned about kidnapping me.

I straightened my spine. No matter what he said, I was his hostage now. In a few minutes, I would become his wife, but I would never be anything more than a captive to my new husband.

CHAPTER 3
LUCA

My palm prickled with the remembered heat of her round ass flushing red beneath my punitive hand. I might not want to get married, but my bride was undeniably lovely. It wouldn't be a hardship to have her in my bed.

And the way she'd become aroused by my discipline...

Yes, my wife and I would get along well. Once she learned to obey. Once she learned that I could offer her pleasure and safety. She would have no reason to resent me if I flooded her lush body with ecstasy every night.

I took a breath and suppressed the lust that'd been threatening to overwhelm me ever since I'd taken her over my knee in the car. Now wasn't the time to ravage my pretty new wife. That could come after the ceremony and then we could seal our union.

Elenora would be mine. For the rest of our lives. Neither of us had a choice.

A pulse of rage seared my veins, burning away some of my arousal. Dante had tried to steal my birthright from me, so I'd been forced to steal his bride. His alliance with Giuseppe Ricci wouldn't go forward. I would've preferred to kill them both, but I wouldn't start a war. Too many of our men respected Giuseppe, my father's most trusted advisor. I wouldn't tear apart my organization before I even took control. My father was on his deathbed, and the Russians were already circling like vultures, waiting to pick away at our territory if we showed any signs of weakness.

So, I found myself in this clusterfuck of a situation: forced into marriage years before I would've considered taking a bride. I'd always known I would have to secure my legacy one day, but that'd been at least a decade in the future. I was barely twenty-eight; too young to be shackled to one woman.

I gritted my teeth and glanced over at Elenora.

Her cheeks were pale and her posture was stiff, but she was still beautiful: willowy and graceful, with a lush mouth that begged for a kiss.

I resented the fact that I'd never fuck another woman ever again, but I valued loyalty above everything else. During my youth, I'd watched my father cheat on my mother half a dozen times, and it'd broken her heart. She'd been so distraught that she'd turned to another man for comfort, and that choice had condemned her.

Ultimately, infidelity was the reason I no longer had a mother. I wouldn't do the same thing to Elenora, who'd done nothing to deserve any of this.

You're a brute. Her hissed accusation snaked through my mind.

Yes, I could be brutal. I had plenty of blood on my hands, and I wouldn't hesitate to defend what was mine.

Elenora was mine, whether she liked it or not. I would never harm her, but I would do what was necessary to keep her in line. It was for her own good. I would protect my fragile young wife, no matter how defiant she might be.

I glanced over at her again. Her spine was straight, her chin lifted. She walked by my side with graceful, sure strides that matched my own as we made our way down the long corridor to the ballroom in my family home. Her slight body might be utterly breakable, but I got the impression that Elenora wasn't fragile. Another woman might've dissolved into sobs after being kidnapped and spanked. My bride held her head high and faced her fate with dignity.

Despite everything, a satisfied smile tugged at the corners of my mouth. Yes, she would make a good wife for me. She would be my queen, a woman I could be proud to have at my side. She was lovely and poised, and she hadn't broken beneath my hand, even if she had bent to my will.

We reached the ballroom doors, and I gently gripped her elbow to remind her not to try anything foolish. In a moment, we would be before the officiant. There was no time for tears or arguing.

She jerked slightly beneath my touch, and I firmed my fingers around her arm. She sucked in a breath, and her lovely hazel eyes flicked to mine. The rich brown of her irises was brightened with striations of soft green, a fascinating pattern that I would study at my leisure when I had her bound to my bed. Her thick, dark lashes swept her brows as she stared up at me, eyes wide with shock. She was still struggling to process her new reality.

I understood. I hadn't planned to marry until I'd discovered Giuseppe and Dante's treachery only a few hours ago.

My thumb brushed the bare skin of her upper arm, and her flesh pebbled beneath my touch. I wasn't sure if her shiver was one of revulsion or a primal feminine response.

I shook my head and looked forward once again, breaking away from the puzzle that was my pretty bride. I had a lifetime to learn every nuance of her expressions. There was no time to linger now, no hesitation.

"You'll be fine, Elenora," I rumbled. "I'll take care of you."

Her slender arm stiffened in my gentle grip. She didn't believe me.

I would just have to prove my intentions to her after the ceremony. Once I had her in my bed, I would show her how good it could be between us.

Forcing my full attention back to the task ahead, I pushed open the door and revealed the opulent ballroom where we would seal our fate. Only three people waited for us: the officiant and my two best men, Lorenzo and Gabriele. They'd driven in the car ahead of us and had arrived first; my closest friends had accompanied me to steal Dante's bride.

Truly, it was a stroke of luck that we'd found her outside her house. It'd saved us the trouble of going in to get her, which could've turned violent, no matter my intentions. And I wasn't at all certain that I would've had the willpower to prevent myself from attacking Dante and Giuseppe if I'd laid eyes on the traitors.

But we were fortunate, and no blood had been spilled.

I led Elenora toward the makeshift altar, her heels clicking across the marble floor and echoing through the empty, cavernous space. Once we sealed our union, I'd host an elaborate wedding reception, and the ballroom would be full of my allies—and my enemies who would've stuck a knife in my back. Even Giuseppe would be invited, and if he was smart, he'd keep his attempted coup a secret from my father.

I had no intention of telling my old man that his best friend had tried to betray his dying wishes for me to take control of our organization. Dad was too frail to even come downstairs for this ceremony. News of the scheme would be a dagger in his failing heart.

This wedding would bind Elenora—and Giuseppe—to me, and the whole affair would be forgotten.

My fingers firmed on Elenora's arm as I thought of Dante. I wouldn't forgive and forget his treachery so easily. I'd keep a close watch on him, possibly even eliminate him after my father passed and I took full control. But until my rule was established, I wouldn't risk destabilizing the organization by murdering one of our most powerful capos. No matter how fiercely I wanted to watch the sadistic light leave his eyes.

We reached the head table at the far side of the ballroom, where fresh flowers were usually kept even when no one was using the space; my home was always kept in meticulous order. The pale pink blooms would have to be decoration enough for Elenora. She'd probably long dreamed of an elaborate wedding ceremony, but the four dozen roses were all that she would get today.

I frowned and decided to make more of an effort for her reception. She might not want to be my wife, but I would prove to her that I wouldn't mistreat her as long as she behaved herself. She was being remarkably docile now, eyes downcast so that her dark lashes swept her too-pale cheeks.

I wished I could see her lovely eyes, but at least she wasn't screaming or railing at me anymore; the spanking had tamed her for the time being.

The memory of her submission and pert ass bouncing beneath my hand sent a fresh pulse of lust through my body, and male satisfaction warmed my chest.

Yes, we could learn to get along well.

"Ready?" Lorenzo asked, dragging my attention away from my bride.

I glanced at my friend and nodded. Like me, he wasn't dressed for this occasion. In fact, he and Gabriele were even more dressed down than I was. The two brothers—nearly identical with their black eyes and thick dark beards—wore simple t-shirts and jeans. I'd at least worn my usual button-down shirt, even if I was also in jeans.

This definitely wouldn't be the fairytale wedding women like Elenora no doubt dreamed about, but it would have to do. Despite the fact that she was dressed in a simple black skirt and sleeveless white blouse, she still managed to appear composed and poised; the same way she'd always looked when I'd seen her at her father's parties over the years. I'd have to be blind not to have noticed her beauty, but she was always too young and too demure for me. I liked a challenge, and I'd expected Elenora to be meek and quiet.

She was certainly docile now that I'd taken her in hand. But she'd fought me in the car. She'd been fiery in her defiance.

I shifted my grip on her elbow and took her hand in mine. Hers was so much smaller, her fingers long and delicate. They were too cold, so I brushed my thumb over her knuckles to warm them. Her remarkable eyes flicked to mine, wide with trepidation and a hint of confusion. She didn't understand yet that as my wife, I would kill to protect her. She had nothing to fear from me.

The short, aged man before us began to drone on, the officiant sounding almost bored as he recited the marriage ceremony like a well-worn litany. Judging by his wispy white hair and breezy demeanor, he'd done this countless times.

Good. I didn't know where Gabriele had found this man or what he'd offered him to oversee this quickie wedding, but clearly, it'd been enough to satisfy the officiant. He hadn't asked any questions, until he uttered the most important ones.

"Do you, Luca Vitale, take Elenora Ricci to be

your wedded wife, to live together in marriage? Do you promise comfort her, honor her, and keep her for better or worse, for richer or poorer, in sickness and health, and forsaking all others, be faithful only to her, for as long as you both shall live?"

Her hand trembled in mine. I firmed my fingers around hers to still their shaking, reassuring her without thinking.

"I do." I sealed my fate with two words, promising myself to one woman for the rest of my life.

"Do you, Elenora Ricci, take Luca Vitale to be your wedded husband, to live together in marriage? Do you promise to obey him, honor him, and keep him for better or worse, for richer or poorer, in sickness and health, and forsaking all others, be faithful only to him so long as you both shall live?"

Her tanned cheeks paled, and her throat worked, as though she was choking on the vow. Her lashes were lowered, hiding her eyes from me.

"Look at me," I murmured, punctuating the gentle command with a squeeze of her hand, grounding her to me. Her hazel eyes met mine, and she blinked rapidly to clear away the sheen of tears. But it was too late; I'd seen the sign of her distress that she was so desperately trying to hide. Her back was straight, her shoulders stiff. Her white teeth sank into her pillowy lower lip to stop it from quivering.

"I'll keep you safe," I promised. "As my wife, you'll be protected. I will provide for you, Elenora. I swear."

I couldn't promise her happiness; only she could make that decision. But I would do my best to ensure she experienced pleasure in my hands. I certainly expected to find my own pleasure in her gorgeous body. I had no intention of remaining celibate for the rest of my life just because my wife didn't want me.

I'd scented her arousal in the car. Some part of her did want me. I could exploit that. She would learn to crave my touch.

"Make the vow," I prompted when she didn't say anything, keeping the words locked behind those lush lips.

She dropped her eyes again. "I do," she whispered, binding herself to me forever.

If the officiant found it odd that I'd commanded my bride to pledge her fidelity, he didn't say anything. Instead, he droned on. I accepted a ring from Nora—provided by Lorenzo

—and slid another onto her finger, along with a massive princess cut diamond engagement ring. My friend had chosen a style well suited to poised, elegant Elenora.

"You may kiss the bride." The officiant finalized the ceremony.

Her eyes were suddenly on mine again, sparking with defiance. Her chin tipped back, a refusal that I took as an enticing challenge. Her teeth flashed in a small snarl, a warning that the little kitten might bite if I dared to approach.

But I dared. I wanted to take a kiss from my spirited bride. I wanted to tame her, to make her melt.

I moved before she could jerk away, hooking one arm around her lower back to trap her against me. My other hand threaded through her long, silken hair at the nape of her neck. I twined my fingers in the chocolate strands, tangling them around my fist. I tugged sharply, and her lips popped open on a shocked gasp as I quickly took control of her willowy body.

I wanted to savor the trepidation in her wide eyes, but I didn't waste my moment of opportunity; I had to seduce her while she was off-balance, or she might change her mind about using those teeth to bite.

My mouth descended on hers, demanding and unyielding. My lips caressed hers with enough force to make them swollen and sensitive. She stiffened in my arms, so I clenched my fist tighter in her hair to command her full carnal attention. I traced the line of her pillowy lower lip with my tongue, a soft contrast to my initial onslaught. She shuddered against me, and her head dropped back slightly, allowing me to claim her more deeply.

A savage, triumphant sound rumbled from my chest into her pliant mouth, and I stroked my tongue against hers. She was hesitant at first, and I wasn't sure if it was from fear or inexperience. Both possibilities sent lust punching through my body, desire flooding my veins. I liked the prospect that my bride was untouched, that she would be mine and mine alone. I could introduce her to all the dark pleasures I enjoyed, mold her into my perfect, sweetly obedient wife.

And I wanted her fear—just a little thread of it. I wanted her to look up at me with those wide eyes as she knelt before me, trembling because she didn't know what I would demand of her next. I would earn her respect even if her love was an impossibility, a fantasy that didn't exist in our world.

She wouldn't love me, but she would submit. She would surrender her will and her body, and I would ensure that she enjoyed every ecstatic second of her submission.

Someone loudly cleared their throat, breaking through the haze of lust that clouded my mind. I remembered myself, my surroundings. I'd just married Elenora, and there were more formalities to handle before I could carry her upstairs and consummate our union.

I broke our kiss and almost released her entirely until she sagged against me, trembling. My arm firmed around her waist, holding her upright. Her gaze was slightly glassy as she stared up at me, her lips glossy from my savage kiss. An arrogant, slightly cruel smile tugged at the corners of my mouth.

Yes, we would get along just fine.

CHAPTER 4
NORA

Black ink shone starkly on white paper as I finished signing my name on the marriage certificate. I felt the seal of my signature on my soul: a damning brand.

Married. I was married to Luca Vitale.

This brute of a man who'd spanked me and stolen a ruthless kiss was now my husband. Only an hour ago, I'd been engaged to Dante Torrio, a notoriously sadistic capo who'd strangled a man right in front of me.

Which fate would be worse? Which man was more of a monster?

It didn't matter now. I no longer had a choice. I never had. I'd always been destined to marry someone who was chosen for me. Love had been a foolish fantasy that I'd allowed myself to indulge, and the loss of that dream knifed through my chest.

The paperwork was signed, the ceremony complete. It was done.

Before I could draw in a shuddering breath, Luca's strong arms closed around me, lifting me up to cradle me against his chest. I stiffened and squirmed, some of my defiance resurfacing; an instinctive, involuntary reaction to being carried off by a brute.

His arms firmed around me. "Calm down, kitten. I'm not going to hurt you."

"Where are you taking me?" I hated the way my voice hitched on the question.

His ochre eyes pinned me deeper into his hold. "You know where we're going, Elenora. Don't worry," he said before I could fully process the implications of his words. "I'll make sure you enjoy it."

I crossed my arms over my chest, as though that would be enough to shield me from the horror of his plans for me. "You're going to force yourself on me." The accusation was sharp, and I hoped it was needles on his soul. I wanted him to hurt for what he was about to do to me.

His jaw ticked. "You will submit, Elenora. And you will love every second of it. You'll come to crave my touch. You're my wife, and I'll make you feel so much pleasure that you'll never want to leave my bed."

"You're delusional," I hissed, tightening my arms over my chest to protect my heart. It would be impossible for me to enjoy anything he did to me.

The awful memory of my traitorous arousal when he'd spanked me snaked through my mind. My stomach turned, and I swallowed against the sudden burn at the back of my throat. Fear fluttered in my chest as he locked me in his dark, unyielding stare and carried me up the stairs with steady, sure strides.

I wasn't afraid that he would beat me; I was afraid that I would enjoy it, just as he promised. I didn't think my pride could bear it. I'd managed to maintain some dignity during the forced wedding ceremony, but I didn't think my spirit would survive this.

"No, kitten," he refuted calmly. "I'm not delusional. You can try to fight me if that makes you feel better, but I have no intention of allowing my bride to remain a virgin. We will share a life together now, and that will include sharing a bed. You'll come to crave my cock." He brushed his thumb up and down my arm, soothing. "I understand if you're afraid. But I'll take care of you. There will be pain the first time, but I'll make sure you feel pleasure too."

My cheeks burned at the mention of my virginity. Of course, he would know that as Giuseppe Ricci's daughter, I'd been sheltered from men. Had he been able to tell that our kiss to seal our union had been my first?

A tremor raced through my bones. Luca would be my first everything. As my husband, he would claim me in every way, and there was nothing I could do to stop him. He was so much stronger than I was, and I knew it would hurt far more if I refused to allow him to claim me as he wished.

I dreaded the shame of experiencing pleasure when he didn't intend to give me a choice, but I would get through this with as much dignity as I could muster. Just like I'd done in the car, I could choose to endure. I wouldn't let him break me.

We stepped into an opulent bedroom, and he kicked the door closed behind us. I jolted as the noise boomed through my entire body, as though he'd slammed it with all his strength. The sound was a condemnation, a punctuation that put an end to my life before this forced marriage. He'd already taken away my freedom to choose my future. In a few minutes, he would take my virginity too. If I didn't carefully guard the core of myself, my soul, he would take everything that I was and strip me down to nothing.

He finally set me down on my feet, his big hands bracketing my waist as though I would fall if he didn't steady me. Embarrassingly, I realized my knees were shaking. I did need the support. I clenched my jaw to keep my teeth from rattling, and a chill settled deep inside my bones. I didn't want to show fear, but terror iced over my limbs despite my best efforts to deny it.

A big hand cupped my frigid cheek, and his warm brown eyes were almost kind as he looked down into mine. "It's okay, kitten. I'll make you feel good."

"That's what I'm afraid of." I whispered the confession before I could think better of it.

A frown tugged at his lips. "There's no need to

fear pleasure, Elenora. I'll show you how good it can be between us. I'll show you what your body is capable of. All you have to do is yield, and I'll make you come so hard you forget your own name. You'll be screaming mine soon enough."

Another tremor wracked my body at his dark promises. The thought of him having that much power over me was terrifying. I didn't want to forget my own name. I didn't want to lose control of myself.

His hand cupped my nape, long fingers sliding into my hair. He tugged gently, urging me to drop my head back, so I had no choice but to stare up into his eyes. My breaths came quick and shallow through parted lips, and his gaze darkened as it flicked to my mouth.

"Don't be afraid, kitten," he murmured, the soft command warm on my cheeks as he lowered his face to mine. "I'll take care of you."

"I can take care of myself." The defiant words came out in a strained whisper. I wasn't sure if I believed them. Not when his strength surrounded me, his huge body caging me in. No man had ever touched me, and now Luca was handling me as though he owned every inch of my body.

His face dipped closer to mine, until our lips

brushed. "You don't have to take care of yourself anymore. I'm your husband. It's my job to protect you. It's my job to give you pleasure. And I'll teach you to please me as well."

Before I could ask him what he expected of me, his mouth descended on mine. The kiss was firm but slow, coaxing me to respond. I fumbled for a few seconds, unsure how to move my mouth against his. I should've turned away from him, but his hand in my hair held me firm. I had no choice but to accept his kiss or turn to violence, but he would easily win if I physically challenged him.

I wouldn't give him the opportunity to beat me and truly break me down. I would kiss him on my terms.

Tentatively, I began to shape my lips to his. When he'd kissed me after the wedding, my lips had parted on a shocked gasp, and he'd plundered my mouth until I was breathless and dizzy. This time, I opened willingly, learning how to meet the teasing strokes of his tongue.

His low rumble of masculine approval rolled into my mouth, vibrating down through my body and resonating deep inside me. A strange, purely feminine warmth I'd never felt before flooded my belly. I liked that he'd made that sound for me.

Despite the fact that he was fully in control, a small pulse of power thrummed through my veins.

He released my hair, his fingers trailing along the side of my neck, tracing the shell of my ear. Sensation lit up my nerves, and sparks raced over my skin at the light contact. I hadn't known a man's brutal hands could feel so decadent.

His touch trailed lower, finding the top button on my blouse. I stiffened slightly when he deftly freed it, so he stroked his tongue deeper into my mouth, claiming my full attention. There was no more teasing, no coaxing; he devastated me. My hands flew to his shoulders, clutching onto him as my head began to spin. There was only his heat, his strength, and his masculine scent suffusing my senses. I didn't have room in my brain to fully register the small thrill of fear as he parted my shirt, and cool air kissed the bare skin of my stomach. My flesh felt too hot in contrast, my body burning beneath his confident, masterful hands.

He found the zipper at the side of my skirt and slowly drew it downward, until the garment loosened and slid down my legs. Instinctively, I tried to twist away and clutch at the fabric to cover my modesty, but his hands shackled my wrists, pinning them at the small of my back as he kissed me with such harsh passion that I couldn't breathe.

He overwhelmed me, stealing the air from my lungs until my head was spinning. When he was satisfied that I wouldn't struggle again, he released my wrists so that he could slide my open blouse down my arms, leaving me in nothing but my simple white bra and panties.

Finally, he broke our savage kiss, allowing me space to draw in desperate, panting breaths. Keeping me locked in his rich brown stare, he reached behind me and unclasped my bra with smooth ease. My skin pebbled when he guided the straps off my shoulders, baring my breasts to a man for the first time.

My hands flew to my chest, covering myself as heat rushed to my cheeks. I had a split second to quiver at his frown before he lifted me up over his shoulder. He carried me across the room, and I heard a drawer sliding open and thudding closed once again. I clutched at his shirt as the world spun, but before I could get my bearings, he tossed me down on his bed. All the air whooshed out of my lungs when my back hit the soft mattress, and he took advantage of my disoriented state. He drew my arms above my head, and something cool and unyielding encircled my wrists. The metal clicked into place before I had a moment to register what he was doing to me. In a matter of a few racing heartbeats, I was trapped beneath him.

I twisted my head back so that I could assess what he'd done to me. Silvery handcuffs glinted around my wrists, the chain connecting them looped around an iron slat on his headboard. A whimper eased up my throat, and I jerked against the restraints. Bruising pain flared beneath the surface of my skin, and terror spiked through my heart.

Luca grasped my jaw, his big hand cradling my face so that I was forced to look up into his deceptively lovely eyes. Thick, dark lashes framed their ochre depths, and their incongruous beauty turned my stomach.

"Don't fight me, Elenora." He stroked my hair back from my cheek almost tenderly, like he was soothing a spooked animal. "This will be easier for both of us if you don't struggle."

"Let me go!" I twisted violently against the restraints, and the cuffs bit into my skin. Fear was a copper tang at the back of my tongue, and panic clawed at my brain.

His weight settled over me, pinning me even

more deeply into the mattress. My primal shriek morphed into a shocked cry when his hand cracked against my breast, lighting up my sensitive flesh with a flash of stinging heat.

"Don't fight me," he repeated, punctuating the calm command with a twin slap to my other breast.

I stopped pulling against the cuffs. Continuing to struggle would only earn me more pain.

"Good girl," he praised, brushing his thumbs over my tight nipples.

Sparks danced beneath his touch, lighting up my body in ways I'd never known before. I bit my lip against a shocked gasp as my clit tingled in response.

"Stop," I begged, burning with humiliation and something hotter that I didn't want to acknowledge.

He lowered his face to my chest. "No." His refusal was a rush of heat over my nipple just before he drew the peak into his mouth.

I barely suppressed a soft moan as his tongue flicked the tight bud, teasing and licking. His teeth lightly scraped me, sending a zinging line of pleasure straight to my sex. Something pulsed at my core, and my clit throbbed in time with the beat of my heart. My breathing stuttered.

"So sensitive," he murmured, his voice rich with satisfaction. "My pretty bride."

He turned his attention to my other breast, his fingers toying with the first as he repeated the decadent torment with his mouth.

"You're a monster," I whispered, my eyes stinging even as my body sang for him.

"No, I'm your husband." He speared me with his dark stare, his handsome features twisted into something fierce and possessive. "You're my wife. From now on, you'll share my bed. In every way. And you will love every second of it. I won't allow any shyness or modesty to come between us. You're mine, Elenora."

I wanted to rail at him that shyness and modesty had nothing to do with it; what he was doing to me was a barbaric violation. He was turning my own body against me, forcing me to feel pleasure when I should feel nothing but revulsion.

I swallowed down the accusations, recognizing the uncompromising glint in his eyes. Arguing with him would get me nowhere. He would only strip away even more of my dignity if I continued to defy him.

I thought of the low, masculine hum he'd made when I'd kissed him back. It'd been an involuntary sound of pleasure, and for just a moment, I'd felt strangely powerful.

I took a breath and gathered my courage. If he intended to make me come undone, I would do the same to him. I wouldn't allow him to hold all the power in this twisted relationship. He was right: he was my husband, and I couldn't change that now. We would share this bed. I could let the awful reality of it break me, or I could learn how to make him weak too.

Something must've shifted in my expression, because Luca nodded in approval and pressed a kiss to my sternum. He traced the line of it with his tongue before moving lower, drawing a hot trail down my stomach. My lower lips tingled as he neared my underwear, and wet heat slicked my inner thighs. I pressed them together as though I could hide the embarrassing sign of arousal, but that only stimulated my sensitized sex.

His white teeth caught the band at the top of my panties, and I stopped breathing as he tugged them down my mound. He kept his eyes on mine, pinning me with his gaze while he slowly peeled away my underwear, baring me to him completely. When he'd stripped me down to my thighs, he gripped the white panties in his fists and jerked them down my legs. To my shock, he shoved them into his pocket rather than tossing them aside, as though he was keeping a perverted trophy.

He loomed over me, fully clothed while I was totally naked and bound beneath him—like a virgin sacrifice to a jealous god. He stroked his hand down my side, caressing the curve of my body. Rough callouses lightly scraped my skin, making my nerves jump and dance for him.

"So beautiful," he rumbled, his fingertips trailing between my thighs to swirl in the slick arousal that painted them. "And so wet for me. Let's find out how good you taste, kitten."

I flushed all the way down my chest. Surely, he wouldn't...

I couldn't hold back a soft cry when he pressed a firm kiss to my clit. He licked the line of my slit, and his low groan vibrated into my core. Through the wash of pleasure, that small sense of power pulsed in my chest once again. He liked the way I tasted. He liked kissing my sex, even though I never would've imagined that powerful, arrogant Luca would ever pleasure a woman this way.

Even in my most secret fantasies in the years I'd harbored a crush on him, I'd never envisioned him as the type of man to enjoy this particularly hedonistic act. I'd always thought there would be something slightly subservient about a man going down on me, but there was no trace of submission in Luca's glinting eyes. He wanted to do this to me, and he would take every ounce of pleasure that he could wring from me.

I was no longer confident that I held any power over him at all. The heat in his gaze and the hungry strokes of his tongue told me that he was finding pleasure in my body, but I had no control over that. His thick fingers clamped my thighs, spreading me wide so that he could feast on me in the way he wanted. I tugged against the cuffs, an involuntary reaction; for an insane moment, I wanted to twine my fingers in his short sable hair and pull him closer.

He growled and nipped at my inner thigh in reprimand for my struggles. I stilled on a gasp, quivering in his bite.

Pleased at my surrender, he licked the imprint his teeth had left in my skin, and sparks danced along my clit in response. His dark stubble rasped over my thighs, a tingling burn that warmed my heated core. He licked at the fresh wash of arousal on my sex, groaning his satisfaction at my responsiveness.

His attention returned to my clit, teasing and tormenting me with his mouth as he slid one finger into my tight channel. I gripped him hard, my inner muscles drawing him in deeper. I'd never been penetrated before—not even by my own fingers—and there was a slight burn that accompanied the ripples of pleasure.

He found a secret spot at the front of my inner walls and crooked his fingertip against it. Bliss burst through my sex, rolling up from my core to flood my entire being. His low, satisfied chuckle rumbled over my clit, and I cried out, arching into him.

I no longer worried about the power he held over me. I no longer feared his touch. All I could do was brace for the waves of pleasure that crashed through me as he caressed that spot inside me and tongued my clit. He eased a second finger into my sex, and there was no pain at the stretch to accommodate him this time; I was too swept up in ecstasy to feel any discomfort.

He continued to stroke me through the orgasm until my thighs shook and my breaths came in gasps. I'd never experienced a release so intense, and the shock of it blanked my mind for a few blissful minutes.

While I languished in residual pleasure, he carefully withdrew from me and stood. I stared up at him as he quickly stripped off his clothes, revealing his powerful body that I'd secretly wished to see so many times. Muscles rippled as he moved, corded arms flexing and abs tightening. His chest might've been carved by a master sculptor. He was even more breathtaking than I'd imagined.

He grabbed something from the nightstand drawer and turned to face me. My lips were parted on shallow, panting breaths as I simply stared. I'd never seen a man's cock before. Luca's was thick and long, surely too big to fit inside me. He fisted the hard length and sheathed himself in a condom. I licked my lips, watching him with growing apprehension. He would try to thrust into me, and it would hurt.

He settled his body atop mine, a weight that should've felt suffocating but was oddly comforting in the wake of my intense orgasm. I liked the reassuring feel of his bare skin on mine, the caress of his hand on my cheek. He looked deep into my eyes, studying my soul. I tried to hide myself from him, but my hands jerked uselessly at the cuffs, and I couldn't seem to tear my gaze from his steady caramel stare.

He petted my hair, the sensation sweet and soothing, despite my mounting anxiety. His cock pressed against my entrance, and I tensed as fear coiled all my muscles tight. I didn't want the pain that was to come. His fingers had stretched me, but surely it would be impossible for me to accommodate his size.

"You can take me," he coaxed, the edge of a growl roughening his gentle tone. "Let me in, kitten."

"I can't," I whispered, barely holding back the tears that stung the corners of my eyes. It was all too much; *he* was too much. He overwhelmed me completely, and I clung to my will by a thread.

"Yes, you can." He stroked my hair again, and his thumb traced the line of my cheekbone as though he was memorizing the contours of my face. As though he cared about me. "Be a good girl and relax for me."

I noted the hard set of his jaw, the flash of

determination in his dark eyes. He would take my innocence tonight: our wedding night. My new husband wouldn't allow me to remain a virgin.

I didn't want it to hurt. I couldn't bear it if I fought him and inevitably lost. He'd promised me bliss, and I would take what he offered. I wouldn't spend my life resisting him only to be irreparably broken in the end. He was my husband, the only man I would ever sleep with. If he was going to take ownership of my body, I could at least take something from him in return: my own pleasure.

"That's it," he praised as my body softened beneath his. He trailed his fingers through my hair, continuing to soothe me as he began to press inside me. "Such a sweet little kitten."

I shuddered, the tone of his voice reaching into my core like a rumbling sensation. Heat bloomed between my legs, even as my tight channel struggled to stretch for him. A sharp twinge of pain set my teeth on edge, and he stilled at my soft whimper. I bit my lip to hold in further sounds of distress and squeezed my eyes shut.

His hand cupped my cheek, his thumb hooking beneath my jaw to tip my head back. "Look at me."

I couldn't seem to resist that deep command.

My eyes fluttered open, and I was locked in his intense stare once again.

"I've got you," he promised. "You're doing so well."

Confusion muddled my mind. He was being so tender with me, but he was hurting me. The praise did something funny to my insides, turning them molten. As he continued to pet me, I released a long, shaky sigh, and my body relaxed around the hard intrusion of his cock.

"Good girl." He said the words through gritted teeth, strain tightening his jaw. He was holding himself back for me, giving me time to adjust to the penetration. He truly did want me to enjoy this.

But there was too much discomfort to feel pleasure, a becoming more unbearable with every thick inch that entered me. I whined and squirmed beneath him, but there was nowhere for me to go.

He shushed me gently and lowered his mouth to mine, capturing my lips. The kiss was an encouragement, urging me to trust in him. His hand left my face, skimming down my throat to toy with my breasts. He rolled my nipples between his clever fingers, lighting up my body with the dark pleasure he'd shown me before. Hot lines of lust zinged from my tight buds to my sex, and my inner muscles relaxed slightly.

He eased out of me by an inch, then pushed slowly back in. His cock brushed that sensitive spot inside me, and bliss finally sang through the pain. I bucked beneath him on a gasp, and his lips firmed on mine, hungrier and harsh with his own need.

He began to thrust gently, stimulating the pleasure point while he continued to play with my nipples. I relaxed further, and the wet heat of my arousal eased his penetration. He drove in deep, and my core contracted around him. His guttural groan made warmth pulse in my chest, that surge of feminine power going straight to my head. He wanted me. I was bound and totally vulnerable beneath him, but in this moment, I held my own sway over him as well.

I clung to the sensation, taking ownership of the ecstasy that raced through my body, claiming it for myself. I allowed myself to fall into it, and the last of the pain melted away. My inner walls squeezed him with velvet heat, and he growled out his satisfaction, a primal sound of masculine pleasure. I wanted him to lose himself in me, to surrender some small part of himself in recompense for decimating me.

I parted my legs farther, welcoming him to claim me more deeply. A snarl vibrated against my lips, and his teeth nipped at me. His palm rested on my throat, thick fingers encircling my neck. For a moment, fear speared my lust, but he didn't squeeze; he simply held me in an act of savage dominance. Some animal part of my psyche responded, and I went supple in his grip, yielding to his superior strength.

He increased the speed of his thrusts, lighting me up with bliss until my body was flooded with it. Sweat slicked my skin, and my muscles drew taut with the strain of containing it.

"Come for me, Elenora," he said, the words a rough command.

I unleashed myself, and ecstasy detonated inside me, bursting from my core all the way to my fingertips and toes. I writhed beneath him, mindlessly riding out my pleasure as my ragged cry rang through the bedroom.

"Mine," he growled, a beast claiming me. "All mine."

He drove deep one last time and released a primal roar. I felt his cock pulse inside me, and I knew he was losing himself in me too. The knowledge of his undoing heightened my pleasure, sensation and emotion overwhelming me completely.

I trembled one last time as aftershocks crackled through my core. Then he withdrew from me, and my entire body went limp. I felt heavy but oddly light at the same time, floating but pressed down deep into the mattress. I couldn't move my limbs if I tried, and I didn't want to. I just wanted to remain cocooned in this haze of residual bliss, where there were no worries or fears.

Luca reached above me, and a clicking sound accompanied the metal cuffs falling away. He grasped my hands and lifted them, pressing tender kisses to the pink marks on my skin. The gesture was shockingly gentle and almost reverent. I simply stared up at him, awed at his beauty and power.

This beast of a man was my husband. He'd claimed me in a way no other man ever would, and now he was handling me like I'd given him a precious gift.

He quickly disposed of the condom and settled down beside me, hooking his corded arm around my waist so he could nestle my body against his.

He pressed a kiss to the top of my head, and within seconds, his breathing turned deep and even.

Despite the horrors I'd endured today—despite the terrifying, ecstatic encounter we'd just shared—exhaustion rolled over me, and I followed him into sleep.

CHAPTER 5
NORA

I awoke with a start, instantly sensing that something was wrong. The masculine scent that saturated my senses didn't belong in my bedroom. This wasn't my bed. The sheets were a softer texture, and the duvet was heavier than mine.

I sat bolt upright, and cool air kissed my chest. I was naked. I never slept naked.

Oh, god. I was in Luca's room. In his bed.

No. *Our* bed. I was married to Luca Vitale, and he'd sealed our union when he'd taken my virginity so ruthlessly last night.

I glanced around wildly, taking in my surroundings for the first time; I'd been too terrified to focus on the décor yesterday. The bedroom was a study in rich shades of red—from the burgundy walls to the Persian rug that covered most of the dark hardwood floor. A black leather armchair dominated the far corner of the room, set beside a drinks cabinet. A decanter filled with amber liquid sat atop it, along with heavy cut crystal glasses. Everything about the room exuded masculinity and wealth.

My attention turned to the bed. I'd noted the black metal slats that made up the headboard yesterday—when he'd cuffed my hands above my head, rendering me helpless to resist him as he claimed my body. My cheeks flamed at the memory, and I tugged the sheets up to my chin, covering my nakedness.

I yelped and clutched the sheets tighter when a door opened to my right. Steam rolled out of the bathroom, and Luca appeared at the threshold. He wore nothing but a towel slung low over his hips, his powerful body on display. A dusting of hair darkened his defined chest, tapering into a trail that led down his rippling abs before disappearing beneath the white towel.

He leaned against the doorjamb, and my gaze snapped to his. I flushed all the way up to my ears, knowing that he'd caught me staring at him. He truly was magnificent, even more powerful and imposing that I'd imagined in my most wicked fantasies.

I shook my head slightly, tearing my eyes from his. Those fantasies had brought me low and made me more vulnerable to him than I could've imagined. The pleasure he'd wrung from my untried body was mortifying, especially my arousal when he'd spanked me in the car.

It was horrifically wrong that I'd felt such bliss when he'd claimed me without my full consent. I'd chosen the pleasure over pain, but he hadn't given me a choice when it came to surrendering my body to him.

My *husband*.

He'd forced me into this marriage. He'd kidnapped me and taken away my freedom.

My stomach dropped at the memory of my sister's screams as I'd been carried off by the brute like I was his prize of war. Giana must be terrified for me.

I took a breath and skewered my new husband with a defiant glare. Better me than her. Giana was far too gentle and sweet for this beast of a man. I could endure his ruthless demands, but she would break beneath his onslaught.

His dark brows drew together at my glower. "In a bad mood this morning, kitten?"

"My name is Nora," I snapped, not caring for the diminutive nickname. It reminded me of how I'd melted in his hands last night, and the shame of the memory was almost unbearable.

He cocked his head at me. "You prefer *Nora* over *Elenora*?" His deep voice caressed the more familiar version of my name, and I suppressed a shiver.

I shouldn't have revealed that. He didn't deserve the intimacy of my true name.

He blew out a sigh, clearly frustrated by my prickly demeanor. "I thought we were past this antagonism. Things don't have to be difficult between us."

"As long as I honor and obey you?" I asked, repeating my forced vows with venom.

"Yes," he replied simply. "You will obey me, Nora."

It was so much worse when he used my name. My gnashing teeth cut the inside of my cheek, and I tasted copper on my tongue.

He sighed again. "I have things to do, and so do you. The wedding planner and decorator will be here in less than an hour. You will help them set up."

I blinked at him. "We're already married." I couldn't keep the trace of bitterness from my voice.

He tipped his chin back, making his strong jaw appear even more forbidding. "We're hosting a reception tonight. Try to look less miserable about the arrangement, darling."

Anger heated my chest at the mocking endearment. "And what will you be doing to help, *dear*?" I shot back.

His lips quirked at the corners for a fraction of a heartbeat, as though I'd amused him. "I'm going to invite the most important members of our organization personally. Including your father." His expression darkened. "His scheme with Dante is over. You're mine now."

I stiffened at the possessiveness in his tone. "I'm not an object to be traded," I insisted. "I'm not your property."

His eyes flashed. "And what alternative would you prefer? Dante Torrio? This marriage has saved you from him. I'll keep you and protect you, Nora, whether you like it or not."

"I'm not a possession to be *kept*. I might be your wife, but I don't belong to you."

He prowled toward me, and I shrank back against the headboard. The cold metal drew a shiver to the surface of my skin, contrasting with the heat of my anger. Despite my fear of my husband's raw strength, I lifted my chin and allowed my glower to clash with his.

He loomed over me, leaning in close as his arms bracketed my waist, his hands pressing into the pillows on either side of my hips. He caged me in, close enough that the heat of his own anger rolled off his body to tease over my pebbled skin. He didn't stop until his lips were an inch from mine, his blazing eyes filling my world.

"You are mine, Nora. And after tonight, everyone will know it. No one will take you from me. Not your father. And not Dante. You do belong to me, kitten. Not him."

As he spoke his intense declarations, his features tightened into something fierce and terrifyingly possessive. In that moment, I realized that he hated my father and Dante, and taking me was more than a power play for him; it was a vicious triumph. I truly was a trophy to him, conquered and owned.

Before I could find the words to express my horror and rage, he crushed his lips to mine. I lashed out, shoving at his solid chest. He didn't seem to notice my fury. Or maybe it simply didn't matter to him. He nipped at my lips, demanding that I open for him. I resisted, so he fisted my hair and pulled sharply, forcing a gasp from me. His tongue surged into my mouth, claiming me mercilessly.

Heat flooded my cheeks, my chest, my stomach. It bloomed between my legs, and I hated that my anger was tinged with traitorous arousal.

Before he forced me to melt for him, he released me from his savage kiss, satisfied at my surrender.

"Go get ready," he ordered, his features stern and forbidding. "You have a busy day ahead of you."

He finally pulled away completely, giving me space to breathe. I hesitated, clutching the sheets to cover my breasts. He was staring right at me. If I got out of bed, he'd see my naked body.

"Go on." His deep voice resonated through the room, brooking no argument.

Hating him, I tossed the covers aside and got to my feet. I didn't look at him as I stalked toward the bathroom. When I passed him, stinging pain bloomed on my bottom, and a loud smack reverberated around us. He'd spanked me again. Like a naughty child.

My entire body burned with humiliation and something darker that I refused to acknowledge. I scooted away from him and slammed the bathroom door between us, leaning against it to heave in several deep breaths. The bathroom smelled like his cologne; it saturated the humid air that was still heavy from his shower.

The man filled my senses, was under my skin. I was still sore where he'd buried himself deep inside me. My husband had staked his claim, and tonight, he would show off his trophy. Everyone would know that I was his: Nora Vitale.

∼

One of Luca's guards, Gabriele, had watched me all day, ensuring I was a good little wife and planned my forced reception. I'd performed my tasks with poise and dignity, not betraying an ounce of the fear that made my insides squirm every time I caught sight of the menacing mountain of a man. Just like my father's cruel guards, I was certain Gabriele wouldn't hesitate to beat me if I disobeyed.

So, I had helped plan a beautiful wedding reception. By the time I'd left the ballroom, it was festooned with pink and white roses, and the band was setting up for the evening. Now, I was putting on the last brushes of my makeup, making myself perfectly presentable in my tea length white dress. It was lovely, covered in delicate lace and seed pearls, with a sweetheart neckline that barely hinted at my cleavage. The whole image maintained an illusion of modesty.

It was too late for that. Luca had already claimed my innocence.

The white, demure design was a mockery, a pretty lie.

I fisted my hand around my makeup brush and studied myself in the mirror. I looked flawless, a beautiful doll for my new husband to own. To *keep*.

I pressed my petal pink lips together, swallowing the sourness on my tongue. I rolled my shoulders and straightened, gathering my resolve. Just like yesterday, I could endure this. I could endure anything Luca threw at me; I wouldn't allow him to break me. He could treat me as a possession for the rest of our lives, but I wouldn't lose myself, my identity. What he did to me didn't matter. He wouldn't alter the core of who I was.

I had years of practice at hiding my emotions behind a composed mask. My passion for dance had granted me poise and elegance that I used to shield my true self. If cruel men saw only a pretty, docile girl, they wouldn't try to crush my hidden spirit. I'd slipped up and allowed Luca to see my defiance several times, a mistake I couldn't afford to repeat. Not if I wanted to keep my soul intact.

Mostly, men left me alone because I didn't give them reason to rebuke me. I was able to indulge in my books, ballet, and piano, and I had my sister: my best friend in the world. I wasn't sure what kind of life my new husband planned for me, but I would do everything in my power to keep my individuality. If that meant obeying his commands, so be it. Obedience didn't mean true submission. I would never succumb to him completely.

"Nora." I stiffened at the command in Luca's tone, the way he said my name with such familiarity. "Come in here."

He was waiting for me in the bedroom. I straightened my shoulders and schooled my features to a calm mask before stepping away from the bathroom mirror. I was finished getting ready, anyway, and it was probably time to start receiving our guests.

My breath caught in my throat when I saw him standing in the center of the bedroom, right beside his—our—massive bed. He wore a tux that fit him perfectly, the powerful lines of his body enhanced by the tailored jacket. His sable hair was pushed back off his brow in an effortless sweep, and his dark stubble roughened his refined appearance ever so slightly, making him appear rakishly handsome.

He held out his hand to me, beckoning me toward him. I realized that I'd stopped in my tracks, staring. I swallowed hard and crossed the room to join him, placing my hand in his.

It was only when his fingers closed around mine that I noticed the syringe in his other hand. Alarm thrilled through me, and I immediately jerked away, but he held me fast.

"It's just a birth control shot," he said, his tone low and soothing.

As though that was meant to ease my panic.

Righteous anger spiked my fear. He was taking my choice away from me, taking control of my body and my future.

"Don't look at me like that," he rebuked, his dark brows drawing low over his rich brown eyes.

"Like what?" I tossed back before I could stop myself. "Like you're a monster?"

His jaw ticked. "It's too dangerous for you to get pregnant right now." He spoke with strained calm, as though trying to explain something simple to a small child. "My father is dying, and Dante won't be the last man to try to take what's mine. We have to wait until I'm the boss and no one will dare to challenge me again. Then we can try for an heir."

"An *heir*?" I spluttered. "You mean a baby. A child that I will bear and will be expected to raise."

His expression darkened to something utterly forbidding. "You will provide our child with a loving home."

"Of course I'll love my child, even if his father is a monster." I wanted to be a mother. I wanted someone to love unconditionally, someone to protect and cherish.

And Luca was trying to take that right from me, at least temporarily.

"I won't make our family even more vulnerable by risking a pregnancy right now," he said, voice brooking no argument. "I will protect you, Nora.

Don't make that more difficult than it needs to be."

I scoffed. He kept telling me not to be *difficult*. When he was the one making insane demands of me, twisting my life into something that suit his desires.

His eyes glinted with warning. "Are you going to bend over the bed for me, or am I going to have to make you?"

Hands shaking with rage, I turned from him stiffly and braced my elbows on the mattress. My cheeks flamed when he lifted my skirt and tugged my underwear aside. It took all my willpower not to whimper with humiliation when the needle stung my bottom. I bit my lip and refused to bury my face in the duvet in an attempt to hide from him.

I wouldn't cower. I wouldn't break.

He stroked my skin like he was reassuring a pet. My fingers flexed into the sheets, and I swallowed a growl.

My anger spiked when he dipped two thick fingers between my legs and brazenly rubbed my clit. I tried to bolt upright, but his free hand pressed down on my lower back, pinning me in place.

"Stop that!" I insisted, my voice vibrating with indignant rage.

He slapped my sex, awakening a stinging burn on my tender flesh. I gasped and went utterly still, mind blanking with shock at the casual way he was handling my most intimate areas.

"You will behave tonight. I won't have my wife glowering at me in front of our guests."

He started rubbing my clit again, reaching beneath my underwear this time. It tingled after the sharp slap, and sparks danced through my core as he firmly stimulated the pleasure point. I squirmed to get away from the mortifying sensation, and he pressed down harder on the small of my back.

I was totally helpless in his domineering hands; there was nothing I could do to stop him from touching me however he wished. A shudder rolled through me, a wave of bliss rippling out from my clit to flood my body with tingling warmth.

I squeezed my eyes shut. "I hate you," I whispered, loathing him with every fiber of my being.

"That's your choice," he growled, rubbing me in a demanding rhythm that sent pleasure zinging up my spine to flood my mind, overwhelming me. "Be good, and I'll reward you later."

His fingertips swirled in the wetness between my lower lips, and then he withdrew his cruelly erotic touch entirely. A strangled sound caught in my throat at the sudden loss of sensation, and he released a satisfied hum.

I shoved up off the mattress, finally freed from his restraining hand. I whirled to face him, unable to compose myself and hide my glare. Hatred was a toxic heat that churned in the pit of my stomach.

He met me with a steady stare and lifted his fingers to his mouth. They were wet with my arousal, and he lewdly licked it off like he was sampling his favorite candy.

My body was incandescent with embarrassment, and I tore my gaze from his. I took in a deep, fortifying breath and drew upon all my willpower. Somehow, I managed to school my features into a composed mask, crushing all my volatile emotions into a tight ball and shoving them deep inside my chest.

I straightened my dress with as much dignity as I could muster, then breezed past my cruel husband, making my way toward the bedroom door.

"Our guests are waiting," I told him coolly, not glancing back to acknowledge him or the filthy thing he'd just done.

I would behave myself. Not for some perverse *reward*, but to ensure that he had no reason to humiliate me like that ever again.

CHAPTER 6
LUCA

My bride was truly lovely: supple and graceful in my arms as I guided her around the center of the ballroom for our first dance as man and wife. The warm lighting picked out the golden threads in her chocolate brown hair, making her shine like an ethereal creature, breathtaking and mysterious.

I couldn't make sense of my new wife. She was so responsive in my hands, but she didn't want the pleasure I offered her. I could be demanding, and I understood that some women didn't take kindly to being ordered around. It posed a challenge, and the most savage parts of me liked that about her: she would be difficult to tame, and her surrender would be all the more satisfying.

But there was no trace of submission in her demeanor now. There was no trace of any particular emotion. She simply looked the part of a docile young bride, a soft smile curving her lush lips. It didn't touch her eyes. I'd seen her melt beneath me, and the woman in my arms wasn't the same one who'd screamed in pleasure last night. Her heart was shuttered, her composed mask concealing all emotion.

I didn't like it. As much as I wanted her obedience, I preferred when the harpy was sniping at me, not this pretty doll in my arms.

I hate you. The memory of her venomous words poisoned my thoughts, and I frowned down at her.

The sign of my displeasure had no effect; not a single muscle on her serene face so much as twitched. It was unnerving. Disturbing. It was like she wasn't even here with me.

I firmed my arm around her waist, and she swayed toward me without hesitation, allowing me to lead our dance. There wasn't so much as a flicker of heat in her eyes, and not even a spark of lust passed between us. So different from our combustible chemistry in our bed last night.

My frown deepened.

I'd told her that her own happiness was her

choice, but I found that I didn't want her to hate me. I didn't want to share a life with a woman who loathed me. She'd been enraged by my insistence that she accept the birth control shot, but I'd only been protecting our family.

I hardened my resolve. I would do what was necessary to keep her safe, whether she liked it or not.

We'd only been married for a day. She would soften with time, especially if I continued to flood her body with ecstasy every night. We would never love one another—that was an impossibility—but I would make her happy.

In that moment, I decided that I wouldn't give her choice, after all. My new challenge, my new purpose in life, was to make my wife blissfully content to be mine. I would have everything I wanted: my birthright and a family. She would give me an heir.

Of course I'll love my child, even if his father is a monster.

I struggled to keep the scowl from my face. Yes, I could be monstrous with my enemies, but never with her. I wouldn't repeat my father's sins.

The song changed, and other guests drifted

onto the dancefloor to join us. We'd performed our part. It was time for me to do the far more important work of securing my birthright. I would have to talk to Nora's father and pretend that I didn't want to kill the traitorous bastard.

I placed her hand on my forearm and led her away from the dancers, toward the head table where my father sat with Giuseppe. Dad was beaming at me, clearly pleased with my choice of bride. I'd married his best friend's daughter; why wouldn't he be happy?

He had no idea about his consigliere's treachery. It'd taken all of his strength to come downstairs for this reception. I wouldn't deliver an emotional blow that might stop his failing heart.

We came to a stop across the table from my father and Giuseppe, and their attention immediately fixed on us. Giuseppe's eyes blazed at the sight of his daughter at my side, but the older man made no other move to express his impotent rage. I'd bested him, and he would have to accept his new reality. One day soon, he would serve me, and Dante would be eliminated.

"Elenora, you look lovely." Dad's voice was weaker than ever, his breaths too shallow. He did his best to sit up straighter and study my pretty bride. "I'm so happy you've chosen to marry my son."

I felt her fingers flex on my arm at my father's choice of words. No, she hadn't chosen this. But it hadn't been my preference either.

Other than that small twitch of her hand, Nora's appearance remained composed, the perfect image of a serene young woman who was happy with her fate. Unease stirred in my gut. No, I didn't like this strange side of my new wife. She barely seemed to have a soul, much less a will of her own.

Had I done this to her?

"I'm disappointed that you eloped, Luca." My father called my attention away from my concerns over Nora's behavior. "Even if I am pleased with your choice of bride."

His disappointment needled at me, but I kept my head held high. My father's pride and acceptance meant everything to me, even if there was no love between us. He had strict expectations of me, and I'd worked for my entire life to meet every one of them. I'd been determined to earn my birthright, no matter the cost.

"I didn't want to bother you with a big wedding," I lied smoothly before shooting a sharp look at Nora's father. "Giuseppe offered his daughter in marriage yesterday, and I didn't want to wait. This way, you can see me married."

Dad would witness the promise of the next generation, even if he wouldn't survive long enough to one day meet my son. That would bring him some comfort on his deathbed. For all my father's sins, I respected him, and he deserved a dignified end.

"I'd like a private word with you, Luca," Giuseppe said. He glanced at my father. "I need to talk to him about his responsibilities to my daughter. The wedding happened so quickly that we didn't have time for a proper discussion."

Dad wheezed a laugh, not noticing the tension between me and his best friend. "He surprised you with the elopement too," he surmised, waving his hand to dismiss us. "Don't give him too hard a time, Giuseppe. This is a happy occasion, seeing our families truly united."

I glanced down at Nora, who had remained dutifully silent while the men talked. It was as though she wasn't even a person, a beautiful statue. She'd railed at me for treating her like a possession rather than a woman with her own thoughts and feelings, and now she was acting like no more than a pretty accessory at my side.

Was this her way of psychologically punishing me for how I'd treated her? By making me feel like the bad guy here? Surely, I hadn't actually broken her.

Monster. Her accusation snaked through my mind.

I shook off the dark thoughts. I could deal with my wife's strange demeanor later. If she was trying to be passive aggressive, she would regret it. I valued honesty, and I wouldn't tolerate this kind of deceitful behavior. She wasn't acting like her true self, and I didn't like it.

I would return to her after I finished talking to Giuseppe. For now, I could leave her in my father's care. I glanced along the high table and noted some of her cousins seated farther down. She would have some familiar company in my absence.

Far from satisfied with the arrangement, I removed her hand from my arm and brushed a kiss over her knuckles, playing the part of besotted groom.

"I'll be back soon." It was a promise and a warning. Nora would behave herself in my absence, or she would have a very sore bottom in a few hours.

She blinked up at me vacantly and smiled.

My stomach turned, but I forced myself to release her. I wanted to shake her instead. I wanted her to tilt her imperious chin and tell me exactly what she thought of me, even if the words might sting a little. Anything was better than this vapid doll act.

If I'd broken her...

I couldn't think about it. Not now. If forcing the birth control shot on her had hurt her so deeply, I would hold her and make up for it later, when we had some privacy. And if she was playing some kind of psychological game with me, she'd learn that I wouldn't tolerate being manipulated. My wife would not hate me, and she would certainly not break because of me.

Giuseppe stood, his body slightly stiff from his arthritis. But he was still an imposing man, and meaner than ever in his advancing age. I left Nora, accompanying him as we strolled out of the ballroom and down the hall toward my father's study.

When the door shut behind us, Giuseppe rounded on me. "You little shit."

I strolled to the drinks cabinet and snagged the decanter, pouring a glass of whiskey for myself and then one for him. I held it out to him with my brows lifted, refusing to reply when he spewed insults.

His thin lips pulled back in a sneer, and he crossed his arms over his chest, denying my offering of civility. I shrugged and placed the glass back on the cabinet before sipping at my own drink, as though this was a casual meeting between old friends.

I settled down in a burgundy leather armchair and swirled the amber liquid in my glass. "I'm willing to forgive your betrayal," I drawled, careful to keep the rage from my tone. Anger would make me appear weak, and if I succumbed to my hatred, I might attack the bastard. My loathing was far older than just a day; his sins against me ran deep, and I'd hated him for years.

"Your daughter is mine," I continued, calm and reasonable. I always had careful control of my emotions, and that long practice served me well now. It was what would make me a good boss, a strong leader. I wouldn't become erratic and unpredictable like Dante. Respect could be inspired by stability, not sadism.

My fingers clenched around my glass at the thought of Dante, my rival. The motherfucker.

I smoothed away my scowl before it could twist my lips and kept my full attention on Giuseppe.

"Your scheme with Dante is over," I declared. "Your loyalty lies with me. We'll put this behind us and move forward as a true family. After all, you're my father-in-law now."

"You're not fit to take your father's place," Giuseppe seethed, gnarled fingers curling at his sides.

"No, you just don't want me to because you think I'll eliminate you at the first opportunity." My hands itched with the keen desire to wrap around his neck and do just that. "But we're allied now, whether you like it or not. I won't kill a member of my family, and you won't defy me again."

His hazel eyes narrowed. "Or what? What will you do? Brutalize my daughter?" He shrugged, and my fists clenched with the need to strangle him.

Did he truly not care if I beat Nora?

No, the old bastard didn't give a shit if I hurt her. I should've known. After the way he'd treated my mother, I knew the motherfucker was callous and cruel. I just hadn't expected that indifference to extend to his own flesh and blood.

I sipped my whiskey and leaned back in my chair, drawing on all my willpower to appear unperturbed. "No, I'll divorce her, and your entire family will be disgraced. You will fall out of favor, and your influence will wane. You can't win this, old man."

He jerked back as though I'd punched him in the face. "You wouldn't. It would kill your father if you caused a rift between our families."

I leaned forward, resting my elbows on my knees. "My father is a dead man walking. I'm thinking of the future. I *am* the future. You can fall in line, or you can get left behind. It's your choice."

He gnashed his teeth. "Dante will kill you."

"He can try, but he won't get any help from you. Will he?" I had him cornered, and he knew it.

When he'd tried to arrange the marriage between Dante and Nora, it'd been a signal of his support for my rival. Now that Nora was married to me, Giuseppe's power play was at an end. Any move against me, his own son-in-law, would be seen as a declaration of war, and he would tear our organization apart. He would jeopardize his position of power by weakening our crime family and making us vulnerable to the Russians.

The old bastard wouldn't risk it.

"Don't make trouble for me, and I won't make trouble for you," I told him coldly. "You can keep your money and your influence. Your life will be unchanged. You will bless this marriage, and we will make peace."

I stood and extended my hand between us. My skin crawled at the prospect of making contact with the man I hated most in the world, but I would see this through. I wouldn't lose my birthright because I couldn't control my own emotions. I was stronger than that. Stronger than this motherfucker, who let spite and fear rule him.

He grabbed my hand and squeezed, as though trying to crush my bones. He was too weak to hurt me in the slightest. I reminded myself that I'd handled the threat, and I didn't need to fracture his fingers. I didn't need to wring his neck.

I couldn't.

I released his hand and drained the last of my whiskey from the glass. "I need to see to my bride," I told him, twisting the knife just a little with the reminder that his daughter belonged to me now. My triumph was complete, and Giuseppe would fall in line.

Nora was mine.

CHAPTER 7
NORA

I stumbled through an open doorway to my right and heaved in a gasping breath as soon as the shadows swallowed me. My chest was too tight, and I could barely draw in air. Sitting at that table with Tommaso Vitale and my cousins had been more than I could bear. I'd maintained my composure for as long as I could, but Alberto's hand on my thigh had broken my careful poise.

Alberto, my older cousin, had always made my skin crawl. When we were children, he'd been my worst bully. As we'd matured, his bullying had turned more disturbing, and the way he looked at me when he hurt me...

My stomach lurched, and I doubled over as nausea gripped me. Blindly, I threw out a hand to support myself, and I fumbled as my fingers clutched at the spines of leather-bound books. A few tumbled to the floor, booming thuds rending holes in my tattered composure like gunshots. My hand finally clamped around a cool wooden shelf, and I managed to remain upright.

I blinked hard, forcing my lungs to expand and draw in oxygen. After an agonizing minute, my hammering heart stopped aching against my ribcage, and I managed to breathe. The shadow-draped library materialized around me, and I straightened, smoothing my dress.

I had to return to the ballroom. I'd excused myself, but I'd been gone for too long to have simply touched up my makeup in the bathroom. If I lingered, Luca might spank me again.

I couldn't bear the humiliation. My body still burned from his mortifying touch after he'd given me the birth control shot. He'd primed my body for pleasure and then taken it away, and my core still pulsed every time his big hands brushed my body. Dancing with him had been almost unbearable, but his absence had been impossibly worse.

Not because of my cooled arousal, but because he'd thrown me to the wolves and left me to deal with them alone.

Heavy footfalls approached, stepping from the rug that lined the corridor onto the wooden floorboards of the library. I shrank deeper into the shadows and held my breath. I couldn't let anyone see me like this. I needed another minute to force my serene mask back into place.

"Nora?"

My stomach dropped to the floor. I recognized Alberto's drunken slur. He must've come looking for me and heard the books fall.

Cursing my uncharacteristic clumsiness, I tiptoed farther between the shelves, praying that he would give up and search for me elsewhere. I had to slip back into the safety of the ballroom, where my possessive new husband would ensure that my sick cousin kept his distance.

I hated Luca, but the years of Alberto's abuse had engrained terror and disgust deep in my psyche. I couldn't let him find me, especially not when he was so drunk. The fact that he'd dared to touch my thigh beneath the table at my wedding reception told me that he was beyond reason. I wasn't sure what he would do if he caught me, but it wouldn't be pleasant.

A floorboard creaked beneath my foot, and I cringed.

"I know you're in here." His voice was dark, rumbling with anger. "Where are you, you little slut?"

I reached the end of the row of shelves and dared to peek around the corner. His thick body was an imposing shadow in the doorway, framed by the golden light that flooded the corridor. He was blocking my way out.

I ducked back behind the shelf and drew in quiet, shallow breaths.

His shoes scuffed the floor as he stalked drunkenly toward me. "You let him fuck you, didn't you?" he spat. "Answer me, Nora!"

I jolted at his booming shout, then pressed myself closer to the shelf. If he kept making this much noise, maybe someone would hear. Maybe Luca would come looking for me.

I shook off the foolish thought. Why wish for one monster to rescue me from another? I would have to get out here on my own. I would save myself.

Alberto stumbled down the aisle, and I took my chance. I rounded the other side and darted toward the door. I made it halfway before my high heel turned beneath me. Fear burst through me, and I cried out as my knees hit the floor. I grabbed at the shelf and pulled myself upright, kicking off the traitorous shoes.

But it was too late. Alberto's weight slammed into me, and the shelf rocked at my back. Books thundered to the floor, the booming sound clashing with the crack of my cousin's meaty hand across my cheek. Pain reverberated through my skull, and the shadows darkened to pure black for a few precious seconds.

His hands bracketed my shoulders, thick fingers digging into my upper arms as he shook me. "You're not a virgin anymore, are you?" he demanded as my teeth rattled. "You fucking whore. You always were a cocktease, and now you've let some other man fuck you."

The library swam around me, but I managed to hiss back, "You're my cousin, you sick bastard. We're related by blood. Get your filthy hands off me, pervert."

Pain lit up my face when he delivered another

vicious backhand. "Shut up!" he thundered. "You're the one who's always tempted me. This is your fault." He flipped me around and shoved my aching cheek hard against the books. "You know you've always wanted this, and you let another man have you first. You'll pay for that."

I writhed, struggling to throw off his weight. He leaned forward, and something hard pressed into my bottom. Bile burned the back of my throat, but his hand clamped over my open mouth to smother my scream before I could release it.

His free hand pawed at my breasts, ripping at the delicate lace on my dress. Tiny pearls popped free, pinging against the hardwood floor as he tore away my modesty. My skin crawled beneath his groping touch, and I twisted in his hold. My eyes burned with furious, terrified tears.

His breath was hot on my cheek when he licked one away and groaned like it was the sweetest thing he'd ever tasted. He reeked of stale beer and sweat, and his palm was slick when he grabbed my breast, fingernails digging into my nipple. I screamed and thrashed, but he held me firm.

It wasn't the first time he'd grabbed me like this, but he'd never torn away my clothes before.

He'd never pressed his erection against me and threatened to rape me.

My blood ran cold, suddenly flash-freezing my skin, which had been flaming hot from the exertion of fighting against him. Alberto wasn't just threatening me. He ripped at my dress with violent intent, his drunkenness making his efforts fumbling but no less horrific.

A furious snarl rent the air, and Alberto was wrenched away from me. I gasped and whirled, clutching at the shelves behind me for support. Two darker shadows grappled in the dimly lit library. The larger man tackled Alberto to the ground and reared back to land a vicious punch across his jaw.

The light filtering in from the corridor illuminated Luca's face, twisted with possessive fury. The little breath I'd managed to take in was knocked from my lungs at the sight of his handsome features sharpened by rage—his strong jaw anvil hard and his dark eyes glittering with menace. His huge hands wrapped around my cousin's throat, and Alberto thrashed beneath him, his heels drumming against the floor as he struggled to breathe.

Luca's lips peeled back from his teeth, and he

growled into my assailant's purple face, squeezing harder. Alberto writhed and tried to pry his fingers from his throat, but my husband didn't shift so much as an inch, not even when Alberto landed a wild, weak punch to the side of his head. Luca shook it off and leaned in closer to him, a murderous light in his eyes.

"You touched my wife," he ground out, the words so gravelly they were barely discernible.

Alberto's mouth opened and closed like a fish out of water, but no sound came out other than gagging noises. His heels slowed their staccato beat on the floor, and his arms stopped flailing. My cousin was dying.

I said nothing; I simply watched the violence unfold in numb shock. I didn't cry out to save his miserable life, but I didn't crave his death, either. All I could do was watch my vicious husband choking the life from him for daring to touch me. Everything seemed surreal, my head spinning from the assault.

Alberto went utterly still, and a pained sound tore from Luca's chest as he ripped his hand away from my cousin's throat. Alberto gasped and choked, spluttering as he rolled into a fetal ball.

Alive. Luca had spared him at the last second. I couldn't process it. I didn't know what outcome I'd wished for.

My knees went weak, and I sagged against the bookshelf. I didn't wish for any of this. I wanted to curl into a ball and sob too.

But I couldn't let them see me cry. Cruel men reveled in my fear, my tears. It only incited them to further violence.

I swallowed hard against the lump in my throat and forced my shaking legs to support me. My torn dress slipped when I righted myself, so I clutched the ruined lace to cover my breasts.

Luca was on his feet and in my personal space in a heartbeat. I cringed away from his brutal hands. His arms dropped to his sides, and he stopped a few inches away from me, giving me space to breathe.

"Are you alright?" he rumbled.

I pressed my lips together and forced a short nod. I was as far from alright as I'd ever been in my entire life, but I wouldn't tell him that. He couldn't know how close I was to a complete breakdown. In the last twenty-four hours, I'd been kidnapped, forced into marriage against my will, lost my virginity to a monster, and been attacked by my own cousin.

I willed my chin to stop quivering and straightened my shoulders. Luca lifted his hand to my stinging face, and I flinched.

A frown twisted his mouth, and he pulled away again. "I'm not going to hurt you, Nora."

I choked down a maddened laugh that threatened to bubble from my chest. Of course he would hurt me. Or worse, he'd make me experience pleasure again when all I wanted to feel was revulsion. That was far more devastating than a slap to the face.

Luca opened his mouth to say something else, but Alberto stirred with a groan. Luca rounded on him and delivered a vicious kick to his gut.

"Stay down," my husband growled. "You're lucky to be alive. Tell anyone about what happened here, and you won't be. You'll never see Nora again."

Alberto spluttered, unable to rise even if he'd wanted to.

Satisfied that the threat was thoroughly dealt with, Luca turned back to me.

"I'm taking you upstairs," he told me, the hard

planes of his handsome face firm with resolve. "You're hurt. I'm going to carry you."

I didn't want him to touch me. I wanted to crawl out of my own filthy skin.

But I didn't try to fight him when he gathered me up in his strong arms and cradled me against his chest as though I weighed nothing. I closed my eyes against the shame that rolled over me in a searing wave and clutched my torn dress together at the bodice.

"What's going on?" A stranger's voice asked. I peeked through lowered lashes and recognized Gabriele, my guard from earlier today and one of the witnesses at our sham wedding.

"Alberto Ricci is in the library," Luca said, cold and controlled. So unlike the heated, half feral way he'd snarled at my cousin. "Make sure he finds his way onto the street. He's not welcome in my home."

Gabriele glanced at me, taking in my torn dress and stinging cheeks, which must be red from where Alberto had slapped me. He seemed to understand the basics of what had happened in the library solely by looking at my disheveled state.

"I'll take care of it," he confirmed to Luca.

"Ask Lorenzo to make our excuses to our guests. My bride is unwell."

Gabriele nodded, and Luca resumed our progress toward the stairs, carrying me up to our bedroom in tense silence. His muscles rippled around me with barely suppressed violence, but he handled me as carefully as though I was made of glass.

We entered the bedroom, and he softly pushed the door shut behind us, like he knew that I would jolt if he made any sudden noises. He crossed the room to the enormous leather armchair in the corner and sat down with me in his arms. He settled me over his lap, keeping a gentle hold on me. I realized that my skin was frigid, and I shivered against his warm body. His big hands ran up and down my arms, soothing away the goosebumps.

"I won't let anyone hurt you ever again," he swore, tone low and dark. "I'm sorry I wasn't there in time to stop him."

I blinked up at him and found his ochre gaze focused on something I couldn't see, something far off in the distance. Anger simmered in the depths of his eyes, was apparent in the granite set of his jaw. And there was something like pain in the harsh slash of his mouth.

"You stopped him," I murmured, unsure why I was drawn to absolve my monstrous husband.

His dark gaze focused on me, roving over my stinging cheeks before dipping down to my ruined dress. "Not soon enough." A touch of the growl returned to his voice. He took a breath and briefly closed his eyes, as though mastering his most feral emotions. When he opened them again, he appeared calmly controlled, more like the man who had pledged his eternity to me with solemn determination.

"Has Alberto ever done that to you before?" His teeth flashed on my cousin's name, but otherwise, he remained composed.

I shook my head, distracted from my distress by the puzzle of my mercurial husband. "He's never taken things that far."

Luca's brows drew together. "He's hurt you before." It wasn't a question.

"Yes," I said softly, voice strangely small. I felt very young and far too vulnerable. I hugged my arms around my chest, drawing my ruined dress more tightly around myself.

Luca lifted his hand to my hair, and I barely

suppressed the urge to flinch away from his touch. Instead, I sat stiffly as he stroked his long fingers through the brunette locks in a slow, soothing rhythm. He'd petted me like this last night, when he'd taken my virginity so ruthlessly.

My insides squirmed. The tender touch tempted me with comfort, but I could still feel the taint of Alberto's groping hands on my skin.

"He'll never breathe the same air as you again," Luca vowed.

My breath caught. "Are you going to kill him?"

I didn't know if I wanted to see my cousin murdered. I never wanted him to touch me again, but was I savage enough to wish him dead?

Luca saved me from the internal conflict. "No," he bit out, but his hand remained gentle in my hair. "I can't kill him. He's family now that we're married. But I'll make sure he never comes anywhere near you."

Relief rolled through me in a riptide, strong enough to make my eyes sting. I blinked rapidly to dispel the tears before they could fall.

"It's okay," Luca promised softly. "I've got you. You're safe now."

Yes, I was safe from Alberto. But who would protect me from my husband?

I shivered and pressed closer to his body heat before I could stop myself. He frowned down at me.

"You're cold. I'll draw a bath for you."

"Okay," I whispered, suddenly exhausted. Yes, I wanted to wash the filth from my skin. And I didn't want Luca to keep touching me. It was making me want to cry, and I couldn't risk that. Not in front of him.

He shifted our positions, nestling me in the big chair while he went to pull the duvet off the bed. He tucked it around me and pressed a quick kiss to my forehead.

"I'm not going to let anything bad happen to you," he pledged, rich brown eyes earnest on mine. "I'll take care of you, Nora."

I nodded mutely, unsure what to say. That I was grateful to him for saving me? That I hated him for forcing me into this marriage?

I just wanted to sink into sleep and then wake up from this nightmare.

Mercifully, he left me alone and went to fill the tub. Within a few minutes, soft floral scents wafted through the bedroom. He was drawing a bubble bath for me. The tenderness of the act was bizarre and completely incongruous with the man who'd humiliated me with dark pleasure when all I wanted was to hate him with every fiber of my being.

I shuddered and sank deeper into the duvet, but it didn't chase the chill from my bones. Luca was only in the next room, but I'd never felt more alone.

CHAPTER 8
NORA

Luca's strong arms were around me again, carrying me as though I was incapable of walking the short distance from the bedroom to the bathroom. I considered arguing with him about the arrangement, but exhaustion sapped my mind, and my tongue felt too heavy to snap at him. He'd removed me from the cocoon of the duvet, and the persistent chill had frosted over my skin.

I eyed the bath with longing, breathing in the floral scented steam rising from the hot water. Luca carefully set me down on my feet, his hands on my waist to steady me. He peered down into my eyes, assessing. Whatever he saw there, it made him frown.

His fingers trailed over the goosebumps that pebbled on my arms. "Let's get you warmed up."

He reached behind me, finding the zipper at the back of my dress. All my muscles locked up tight. "What are you doing?"

He shushed me gently. "I just want to help you. Let me."

The command wrapped around my ravaged soul, and I was too tired to defy him. All the fight drained out of me, and I started to go numb. My husband was stripping me. He would get me naked and touch me in ways that made me blush.

I would endure this. I had to.

"Look at me."

Another command. My eyes snapped to his.

He cupped my cheek in his hand, thumb skimming over the heated skin that still prickled slightly from where Alberto had slapped me. I stared up at him blankly, retreating further into myself.

Lines of strain deepened around his eyes. "I'm not like him." A hint of the feral growl returned to his voice, but otherwise, he remained calm and handled me with aching care. "I will never hurt you like that."

I said nothing. He claimed that he wouldn't

violate me, but he was taking off my dress. There was only one thing he could possibly want from me.

His jaw ticked, but his hands remained gentle as he slowly drew down the zipper at the back of my dress. I shivered when the ruined garment dropped to the floor, leaving me in nothing but white lace underwear.

To my surprise, he didn't remove them right away. He retrieved a brush and hair tie from the sink cabinet and quickly returned to me. Curiosity stirred in the depths of my detached state. I didn't understand his strange actions, but I wouldn't fight him. There was no point; he would inevitably win.

I slipped deeper into my composure, allowing my body to become gracefully poised and my expression to relax into something vacant and serene.

"Why are you doing that?" he asked, a sharp edge to the question.

I blinked up at him. "Doing what?"

He gestured at my body, my face. "This vapid doll act. Is it a passive aggressive guilt trip, or have I truly damaged you so deeply?" Those fine lines around his eyes deepened.

"This is how I always look," I hedged, unease tightening my belly. No man had ever noticed that my composed mask was a lie.

His lips pressed into a grimace. "No. I've seen you, Nora. You're far from vapid. You're my wife. I want to understand you, so we can build a life together that isn't miserable. I can't make you happy if I don't know how to read you."

Surprise pierced my unease. "You want to make me happy?" I breathed.

Before, he'd said that happiness was my choice, as though he didn't care one way or another.

He nodded. "I don't want you to hate me. And I won't play games with you. So I'll ask you again: why do you put on that pretty doll act?"

I blew out a sigh. "It has nothing to do with you. I'm a dancer. I'm poised when I perform."

His brow furrowed. "Perform?"

I shrugged. "That's how I always act around men. It keeps me safe."

"What do you mean? What men have made you feel unsafe? Alberto?" He scowled on my cousin's name.

I gaped at him. "All men are dangerous." How could he not know that? "If I ever displease my father, he has one of his guards punish me. Ballet taught me to be serene and composed. I learned a long time ago to draw on those lessons outside of the dance studio. If I don't provoke anyone, they have no reason to hurt me."

I was giving away one of my deepest secrets, making myself vulnerable to him. But somehow, he'd already figured out that my careful composure was a lie. Maybe it was because I'd let him glimpse my defiance far too many times since he'd kidnapped me and taken my virginity. He'd seen beneath the mask, and I couldn't put it back on.

He curled two fingers beneath my chin, tilting my face back so that he could stare deep into my eyes, my soul. "I will never task another man with punishing you," he vowed. "I will never brutalize you."

I bit my lip, thinking of how he'd spanked me. That hadn't been brutal or inflicted lasting damage, but it had effectively chastised me. My cheeks warmed at the embarrassing memory.

He traced his thumb over my mouth, encouraging me to relax. "I'm not like your father, and I'm not like mine." His voice deepened, his eyes darkening. "My father beat my mother so badly that she was hospitalized. She became addicted to opiates after that. Two years later, she died of an overdose."

My heart squeezed at his confession. I'd known that his mother was dead, just like my own, but I hadn't known how she'd died. Luca's admission was shockingly intimate. He'd made me vulnerable, but he was sharing something that made him vulnerable in return.

He cupped my cheeks in both of his big hands, cradling my face like I was precious and fragile. "I will never hurt you like that, Nora. I will not be that kind of husband."

I swallowed against the lump that'd formed in my throat. I was so tempted to believe him. I wanted to believe him.

But I'd spent my entire life fearing men and their violent tendencies. Less than an hour ago, my own cousin had slapped me and tried to violate me.

Luca pressed a tender kiss to my forehead. "You'll believe me one day," he murmured. "I'll prove it to you."

I pressed my lips together, fearful that I'd spill more of my secrets if I dared to reply.

Luca seemed to understand that I wouldn't say anything more, so he stepped away and picked up the hairbrush again. Shock loosened my tight chest when he gently ran it through my hair, careful not to pull at the worst of the tangles where Alberto had mussed it. I allowed him to continue in silence, my mind too muddled to come up with conversation. The act was strange but soothing. The bristles massaged my scalp, and after a few calming, quiet minutes, my hair was glossy and free of snarls.

He gathered up the heavy locks and tied them in a loose bun. I watched him in the mirror in front of me, feeling too shy to meet his eyes directly. A man had never touched me like this: with tender care. There was nothing sexual about the way he was handling me, even though I was mostly naked. Warmth pulsed in the center of my chest, chasing the last of the chill from my bones.

When he was finished, he brushed a kiss over my nape, then dropped to his knees before me. His thumbs hooked through my panties, and I didn't resist as he slowly slid them down my legs. I stepped out of them, and he took my hands in his. Wordlessly, he guided me to the tub.

I sank into the warm water, until the bubbles tickled my chin. Luca rolled up his sleeves, revealing corded forearms. Then he picked up a washcloth and dipped it into the suds. I pulled back slightly when he reached for me.

"What are you doing?" I asked, my voice strangely soft and slow. I felt sleepy and a bit drunk, so tired after everything that'd happened to me in the last twenty-four hours.

"Taking care of you," he replied, as though it was the most natural thing in the world.

He began to wash me, and I didn't protest. It felt strange, but good. Maybe this was normal for married couples? I didn't know anything about what happened in private between a man and a woman. My naivete was a little embarrassing, but I was too relaxed to feel any shame.

"I'm sorry for upsetting you earlier," he said after a while, his voice a deep rumble.

My eyes fluttered open, and I found him watching me with a heavy-lidded gaze, as though he was feeling slightly drunk too.

"When?" I asked. He'd upset me so many times since he'd kidnapped me. *Upset* wasn't even a strong enough word.

"When I insisted you take birth control," he reminded me.

A needle of anger pricked at the peaceful cocoon that'd engulfed me, but he immediately soothed it away with a stroke of the cloth down my spine.

"I think I pushed too hard, but I need you to understand that everything I've done is for your own protection. We can't risk a pregnancy right now."

My cheeks heated at the memory of how he'd humiliated me with his erotic touch after he'd given me the shot; how he'd promised to *reward* me with pleasure if I behaved at the reception.

"And after that?" I asked, still too lethargic for the demand to hold any venom. "When you touched me and teased me. How was that protecting me?"

Another stroke down my spine. I melted into his touch.

He released a low, satisfied hum. "Our marriage has to seem real," he explained calmly. "My position as heir isn't secure if this alliance with your father doesn't seem genuine. If you'd fought with me at the reception, everyone would know that you hate me."

I pressed my lips together. Before the party, I had told him that I hated him. And in that moment, I'd meant it. Now, I wasn't sure of how I felt about my mercurial husband. He'd promised that he wouldn't harm me. He'd sworn to protect me. And he had defended me from Alberto. He was touching me with nothing but tenderness as he bathed me.

I said nothing, too tired to puzzle out my conflicted feelings toward him.

That night, he didn't force himself on me. He didn't wring pleasure from my unwilling body, and he didn't selfishly claim his own. My husband simply held me, cuddling me in our bed and petting me until I fell into a deep, dreamless sleep.

CHAPTER 9
LUCA

I'd been a married man for nearly a week, and I still barely knew my wife. I'd been busy with the family business and with moving my ailing father into our house in the city. He'd insisted on giving the Long Island mansion to "the newlyweds" since I had no plans to take a honeymoon. Tensions were still running high, and Dante hadn't shown his face since I'd stolen his bride. If Dad found his absence at the reception odd, he didn't remark upon it.

Most likely, he hadn't even noticed. He'd barely made it down the stairs to join the party, and exhaustion sapped his senses.

I'd taken note of it. And I was wary that Dante hadn't come to meet with my father once since the wedding. I had no idea what his next move might be. He hadn't declared open war on me, but he hadn't come back into the fold either. For all appearances, he seemed to be running his business as usual. The money was still coming in from his various enterprises, so there was no reason for my father to be suspicious.

I would never trust the sadistic bastard.

So, I'd been working long hours away from Nora, coming home to find her already asleep in our bed. I hadn't fucked her in the harsher way I truly wanted since the night I'd taken her virginity, a delay I wasn't keen to continue. After the reception, she'd been too traumatized by her sick cousin's attack for me to touch her sexually. And in the days since, I'd been more cautious in how I handled her. I'd made sure she experienced pleasure when I claimed her body, but I hadn't been fully satisfied.

I hate you. Every time her acerbic words needled my mind, they dug a little deeper. I didn't want to share my life with a woman who hated me. And I certainly didn't desire Nora's disgust.

On the night she was assaulted by Alberto, she'd shown remarkable strength and resilience. And she'd never once crumpled and sobbed since

I'd kidnapped her and forced her into this marriage. She'd told me that men had beaten her throughout her life, but she still possessed fire in her soul. I'd liked that defiant fire the first time I'd taken her over my knee. I didn't want to be the one to snuff it out.

I'd been more careful with her than I would like since the reception, sparing her from my darker needs. I liked taking care of my pretty bride, but I didn't intend to deny my desires for the rest of my life. She would learn to accept them; I would teach her to love my more deviant plans for her.

I just had to woo her outside the bedroom, and she would be more amenable to trusting me to fuck her however I pleased. This could be a happy marriage, if I could just convince my beautiful wife not to hate me.

She watched me warily as I approached her in the library, sinking slightly deeper into her plush armchair and pulling her book protectively up to her chest. Nora didn't fear me, exactly, but she always tensed when I neared. Particularly now, when I was in a deviant mood. She must've been able to read something darker in my demeanor, because she licked her lips in trepidation and desire.

Perfect. My pretty wife was learning to please me, even if she didn't realize it.

I planned to take another step in her training.

I held out my hand, beckoning. "Come here."

She was breathtakingly graceful when she unfolded herself from the chair and got to her feet. She truly did have a dancer's form. I relished the prospect of admiring her at my leisure. I hadn't wanted to marry, but Nora would be a good companion for me. There were worse fates than having such a striking woman in my bed and at my side.

She looked up at me, curiosity sparking in her hazel eyes despite her attempt to put on the composed mask that I hated. She couldn't seem to help herself; she always tried to hide behind it, a lifelong mechanism for self-preservation.

I could be patient with her. I loved slowly making her come undone as I tempted and provoked her by turns, until the real woman underneath was panting and moaning in my arms.

"I have a surprise for you," I told her, watching every nuance of her expression.

Her eyes sparked before she blinked away the moment of anticipation. An arrogant, satisfied smile tugged at the corners of my mouth. Yes, she would like this. She would love every aspect of what I was about to give her.

"You don't have to give me anything," she murmured, demure behind that false serene smile.

I touched two fingers beneath her chin, lifting her face so that she was locked in my steady stare. "I want to give you things, Nora. I can make you happy. Let me."

Her brow furrowed slightly, the mask starting to crack. "You really mean that?"

She still didn't believe me.

I caressed her cheek. "Why would I want my wife to be miserable?" I reasoned. "We can have a good life together, kitten."

Her lips no longer pursed with irritation when I used the endearment.

My smile widened. She was doing so well.

"What's the surprise?" she asked, avoiding my more serious assertions about our future.

I let it slide. In the short time I'd known her, I'd gotten the sense that Nora didn't allow herself to envision her future. She was in survival mode, living day to day and struggling to adjust to her new reality of married life. She'd spent her time exploring the layout of the mansion and the grounds, and she'd met the staff who ran it. She was learning to manage the household, a task I was certain she would perform beautifully.

But that alone wouldn't fulfill her. I'd found her in the library more than once, cozied up with a romantic novel. My wife would want more from her life than a cold union with a mafia Don, existing solely to keep my home and raise my heir.

I could offer her so much more than that. Not the fantasy of love that she probably secretly dreamed of, but I would provide for her and give her a good life. That was the most anyone could ask for in the real world.

I smiled down at her, my grin a touch wicked. I loved the way she shivered in response.

"If I told you, it wouldn't be a surprise," I chided.

I reached into my pocket and pulled out the length of black cloth. She blinked at it, puzzled. My innocent bride had no idea what I planned for her.

Anticipation coiled my muscles, and my grin sharpened. She swallowed hard, but she tipped her chin back and didn't retreat so much as an inch. Nora was brave and beautiful, a good match for me. I would quickly tire of a wife who crumpled and wept every time I turned this darker side of myself on her.

I lifted the cloth to her face, and she didn't flinch when I brushed the satiny material over her soft cheek.

"What are you doing?" she asked, her voice a touch breathless.

"Trust me," I cajoled, desire already gathering at the base of my spine. I craved her trust, her true submission. She would surrender completely to my will, and she would love every ecstatic second of it.

Her eyes were wide and wary on mine. She didn't trust me at all. Not yet.

That would come with time. For now, I would revel in corrupting my innocent bride.

"Close your eyes," I ordered, tone soft and encouraging. My kitten could be very sweet if I handled her gently. A barked order would make her bristle, and I didn't want to treat her harshly today. This was all about her pleasure, making sure she enjoyed my kinkier games. She would come to crave them as much as I did.

She eyed me suspiciously, but as I lifted the cloth, her lashes obediently lowered to fan her cheeks. I drew the blindfold around her head, careful not to trap any of her glossy hair as I knotted it firmly in place. Her lips parted on a soft gasp, and she shook her head slightly as though to toss the length of cloth away.

I cupped her face in my hands, stilling the sign of defiance.

"It's too late for that, kitten," I told her, leaning in close so that she could feel the heat of my declaration on her neck. "You're mine now."

"I don't like this." Her protest shook slightly, but her voice was low and breathy. And she made no move to fight me off or tear away the blindfold.

She stood stiffly before me, small hands fisted at her sides as though she was willing herself to stillness.

I stroked my hand through her hair in the way that she liked. "You're being so brave for me, Nora. Such a good girl."

She huffed, her pride chafing. "I don't like this surprise."

I nipped at the shell of her ear, and she trembled.

"Liar," I whispered, the truth snaking into her mind.

I wrapped my fingers around her nape, squeezing gently. Her lips popped open on a soft gasp, all her senses heightened now that I'd taken her sight. My arrogant chuckle was slightly cruel.

"But this isn't your surprise," I said, allowing the words to fan her neck with heat. Her sensitive skin pebbled, and I ghosted a kiss over her throat.

A soft keening sound slipped from her, and she quickly pressed her lips together, cheeks coloring with a touch of embarrassment at her lustful response.

"Come with me, kitten."

I eased back, and she swayed toward me. I laughed again, delighted with her responses. She truly was perfect for me.

I took her dainty hand in mine and led her out of the library. Her first steps were slow and hesitant, but not clumsy. Graceful Nora would never be clumsy, even blindfolded and disoriented.

"Where are you taking me?" She tried to issue a demand, but it was little more than a whisper.

I shook my head, even though she couldn't see me. "Has no one ever given you a surprise, Nora? You don't seem to understand how they work."

Her shoulders stiffened, but her steps didn't falter. Every time I needled her, she showed a bit more of her hidden spirit. For a greedy moment, I wanted to remove the blindfold so that I could see her composed mask falling away completely.

But I was enjoying her helplessness too much to ruin the moment. Mastering the fleeting urge, I firmed my fingers around hers and led her the rest of the way down the corridor, to a room at the far end of the west wing. It'd once been a seldom-used, smaller dining room. I'd had it altered just for her, spending a small fortune to make the changes within days. I'd kept this part of the house closed to her, so she wouldn't discover what I had planned for her until it was ready.

I led her into the room and positioned her at the center of it. When I had her exactly where I wanted her, I cupped her nape and tipped her head back to claim a kiss. I started gently, not wanting to startle her with harsh, hungry contact. I traced the seam of her lips with my tongue, and she opened for me willingly, accepting my claim. I kissed her long and deep, until her hands curved around my shoulders for support as her knees went weak.

My base urges told me to continue, to lay her out on the floor and fuck her hard. But that wasn't what I'd planned for her. For us.

So, I forced myself to step away, circling

behind her to unknot the blindfold. I let it slide from her face, and she blinked rapidly to adjust to the sudden wash of light. I knew the moment her sight returned.

The awe that softened her lovely features was breathtaking, and I imprinted the memory on my brain. Nora was all mine, and after this, she'd offer herself to me freely. If she wouldn't believe my pledge that I wanted to make her happy, actions would prove my intentions.

"Luca..." She breathed my name, and it went straight to my head, making me feel slightly high.

She'd never said it like that before, like a prayer.

She turned her head slowly, taking in the floor to ceiling mirrors before us, bisected by a barre.

"This is for me?" she asked, peering up into my face. Her eyes were wary again, as though she didn't dare to believe that I'd done this just for her.

I traced the soft line of her lush lips. "Yes, kitten. It's yours."

"Was it always here?"

"No. I had it built for you."

Her brow furrowed, and she glanced around at the studio. "But you don't even know anything about me."

I captured her chin between my fingers, hungry to watch every nuance of her expressions. "You told me that you're a dancer. I contacted your sister and asked her to send over your things."

Her eyes sparkled, and she blinked quickly. I didn't want her to shove the emotion away, but I didn't press her to fully release the depth of her gratitude. If she didn't want to cry, I wouldn't force her.

"You talked to Giana?" She spoke as though she could hardly believe what I was saying.

How little did she think of me that she was so baffled by my actions?

I didn't like that thought, so I petted her hair and savored the way she leaned into my tender touch.

"Yes," I confirmed. "She packed up your gear for you. It arrived this morning."

I turned her and directed her attention to the chair in the corner, where I'd laid out her dance outfit and pointe shoes.

I leaned down from behind her and kissed her cheek. "I want you to dance for me," I murmured.

That chair was for me. I intended to spend many hours in here watching my beautiful wife perform solely for my pleasure.

I applied pressure at the small of her back, urging her toward the waiting clothes and shoes. "Go on. Get changed."

She peered at me over her shoulder. "Now?"

"Yes, now." I allowed my tone to drop to something sterner, pushing her just a little.

She was malleable after being blindfolded and pleasantly caught off guard by her surprise, so she didn't argue with me. Satisfaction flooded my chest as I watched her practically float across the room to retrieve her outfit.

She hugged the pointe shoes to her chest and closed her eyes briefly, as though savoring the feel of them in her hands.

Then she looked back at me. "There's nowhere to get changed."

I gestured at the mirrors. "You'll change right here. For me."

I prowled toward her, and she shifted on her feet. But she didn't shrink away. I allowed my hand to brush hers as I passed her and settled down on my chair. I leaned back into the plush leather and waved her on, silently commanding her to obey.

She bit her lip, and her cheeks flushed, but she reached for the button at the top of her modest, pale pink blouse. Her fingers trembled slightly as she undid it, then reached for the next.

"Slowly," I ordered, a bite to the command.

Her eyes snapped to mine, wide with surprise at my harsher shift in demeanor. I nodded at her, encouraging her to continue in the way I'd instructed.

Her lashes lowered, shy as she complied with shaking hands. I allowed her to avert her gaze from mine until she was stripped down to her underwear, and she reached for her white tights.

"Look at me. Watch me while you put them on."

She swallowed, but her hazel eyes remained locked on mine as she eased the tights over her long, slender legs. As she slowly complied, my cock stiffened. I kept my hands on the arms of the chair, denying myself. I was in control here; I had an iron grip on my own body as well as on her will.

When she was finished, her limbs were practically liquid as she flowed into her next movement. She stepped into her leotard and pulled the straps over her shoulders, then stood as though a string tugged at the top of her head, lifting her entire frame in an elegant pose.

I picked up the remote from the small table

beside my chair and pressed the play button. Music swelled throughout the studio, the first lilting notes of her favorite number from Tchaikovsky's *The Sleeping Beauty* surrounding us.

Her features softened. "How did you know?"

"Giana told me it's your favorite."

"I..." She blinked rapidly. "Thank you, Luca."

My gut tightened when she said my name with reverence, lust punching through me.

"Now the shoes." A slight growl roughened my voice as I suppressed my most primal desires to grab her and fuck her hard.

She reached for them just as the studio door burst open with a bang. She yelped and lifted her hands to her heart, startled. I was instantly on my feet, positioning my body in front of hers.

Two of my guards stood in the doorway, guns drawn.

One of them spoke, and my blood ran cold. "Your father is dead. You're to come with us. Dante wants to see you."

CHAPTER 10
LUCA

"I don't answer to Dante and neither do you." My words were cold and precise, and I clung to my control by a thread. I couldn't fly into a rage. One wrong move could send bullets flying, and Nora might get hit.

Fear like I'd never known before gripped my lungs with sharp claws, digging deep and robbing my breath. Because I wasn't the only one in danger. My heart hammered against my ribcage at the prospect of my fragile wife being hurt. It was my job to protect her, and now I had two traitors in my home, guns threatening her.

The man who'd spoken first, Andrea, swallowed hard but firmed his grip on his weapon.

"Dante paid us well. He's the boss now. You're coming with us. Quietly, or we won't hesitate to shoot."

"Don't point that at my wife." I couldn't quite keep the growl from my voice.

Both weapons trained on my heart. The second man, Federico, said, "Dante wants her alive. She won't be harmed. He wants to see you both, but we have orders to shoot you if you try to resist."

My mind churned. Dante wanted both of us. Probably to make an example of me. And Nora...

My teeth flashed in a snarl. I knew exactly what that sadistic bastard wanted from my pretty wife.

"You're both dead men," I informed them, struggling to maintain my cold demeanor. "You'll pay for betraying me."

Andrea paled, and his gun swung in Nora's direction. "Come quietly, or I'll hurt her."

Federico swore. "We can't. Dante said—"

"Dante will get over it," Andrea snapped, sweat beading on his brow. "We're getting the fuck out of here. Right now."

He was right to be nervous. They weren't the

only men guarding my estate. If I gave even the smallest signal to any of my people as we exited the mansion, Andrea and Federico would die instantly. They were counting on the threat of their guns to subdue me. But Andrea could see the truth in my eyes: I wouldn't willingly go to Dante under any circumstances, even if it meant risking my own life.

But Nora's life...

No, I couldn't risk her.

I couldn't let Dante have her, either. I couldn't even let myself begin to contemplate what the sick motherfucker would do to her if he got his filthy hands on my wife.

"Alright," I bit out. "I'll come with you. Just keep your aim on me, not her."

I took a slow step forward, and Andrea's gun jerked back to target my heart.

My teeth cut the inside of my cheek when Federico insisted, "She's coming too."

I held out my hand behind me, never taking my eyes off the threat. I couldn't focus on Nora's terror. I couldn't take my attention off the traitors for so much as a heartbeat.

"Get behind me, Nora." I kept my voice

controlled, tone calm. I couldn't spook her, or she might bolt. I needed her firmly shielded by my body.

Her hand trembled when she placed it in mine, and I gave her fingers a reassuring squeeze. I wanted to swear to her that I would never give her to Dante, but there would be time for that later. We wouldn't leave our home with these bastards. Even if it meant taking a bullet myself, I wouldn't let them anywhere near her.

We took slow, measured steps toward the two men, and they eased back into the corridor. When I reached the threshold to the dance studio, I acted. Grabbing Nora's hip, I shoved her farther inside the room, to the left so that she was no longer a target in the open doorway.

"Get down!" I barked, lunging at Andrea first —he'd proven to be the more unstable one, so I needed to handle him quickly.

I grabbed his wrist and twisted, drawing on my years of training to disarm the threat. Two shots boomed through the corridor, one from my gun and the other from Federico's. My bullet ripped through Andrea's skull, exiting in a bloody splatter against the wood paneled wall. Federico's bullet grazed my upper arm, a shot to injure but not to kill; he was still obeying Dante's instructions to bring us in.

It was too late for that. My men would've heard the shots, and they'd be here to back me up in seconds. I had less than a minute to interrogate Federico.

I grabbed his elbow and twisted, forcing him to turn away from me as I popped his shoulder out of its socket. He screamed, and his gun clattered to the floor. I kicked it away and shoved him forward, so that his skull cracked against the wall. A crimson smear darkened the wood as he slid to the ground.

While he was disoriented, I grabbed Andrea's knife that he'd kept hidden in his boot—I'd noted the extra weapon when I'd slowly edged out of the dance studio. I was on Federico in a heartbeat, plunging the blade into his gut. He screamed, back arching in agony.

"Who else on this estate is working with you?" I demanded, my voice loud enough to be heard over his ragged cry, but my tone clipped and controlled.

The threat had been neutralized, and now I needed information.

"No one else!" Federico gasped out.

I twisted the knife. Another guttural scream.

"Tell the truth," I prompted, ice cold.

"It was just Andrea and me," he babbled. "That's all I know. Dante paid us for this a week ago. He's been waiting for your father to die. Please—"

I swiftly withdrew the knife and plunged it back in, tearing flesh and vital organs.

"I'm sorry... So sorry, Luca. I don't know anything. Please, you have to—"

The traitor's pathetic plea was silenced when I wrenched the blade free from his gut and brought it up to his neck in one fluid motion, slitting his throat. Blood sprayed, warming my cheek. It spilled from his ruined throat, pouring over my hand. His mouth opened and closed, his eyes wide and wild. I didn't bother to watch the light leave them. After his betrayal, Federico didn't deserve any company in death.

I tossed the knife away and got to my feet just as half a dozen of my men thundered toward me, rushing to answer the sound of the gunshots. I waved at them to stand down.

"I handled it." I informed them. I toed Andrea's ruined skull. "Clean this up. Find their friends and question them. Dante has declared war."

I didn't wait for them to finish promising to obey. The need to get back to Nora was an itch beneath my skin. I'd pushed her to safety, but two bullets had been fired. If one of them had somehow hit her...

I wouldn't fail her. I couldn't. Not again.

Never again.

I would protect what was mine. Nora belonged to me, and I would slaughter anyone who threatened her.

I turned away from my men and stepped back into the dance studio. Nora was pressed against the wall, knees drawn up protectively to her chest and her arms braced over her head. I'd ordered her to get down, and she had. She'd stayed out of the way while I'd handled the fucking traitors who'd dared to try to take her to my worst enemy.

She looked up at me, eyes wide enough that her long lashes brushed her dark brows. Her gaze quickly roved over my body, assessing.

"You're hurt!" she exclaimed, surging to her feet to grasp my forearm.

I glanced down and found her examining the

angry red burn where Federico's bullet had grazed my upper arm.

I didn't feel any pain; despite my controlled mask, adrenaline churned through my system, the need for more violence setting my teeth on edge. I'd already destroyed the men who'd tried to take her from me. There was no one left to kill.

But my blood ran hot in my veins, and the concern for me that pinched her pretty, delicate features only fanned the flames. My beautiful wife had just been held at gunpoint, and instead of collapsing in tears, she was worried about *me*.

The icy mask I'd worn cracked, exploding as an inferno of emotion surged through me. All the rage I'd felt at seeing her threatened rose up in a searing wave, mingling with the fear for her life that'd twisted my insides. The fire morphed into a primal, possessive heat, and the need to stake my claim over her clamped my mind.

They'd tried to take my wife from me. But I wouldn't let her go. Nora was mine.

I buried my bloody fingers in her silken hair and pulled her toward me, sealing her lips with a fierce kiss. I didn't caress or cajole her this time, not like I'd been treating her so carefully since the night I'd taken her virginity. This was a fierce, animal dominance of my wife, my mate. I fully unleashed myself on her, taking everything that I wanted. She made a small sound of alarm at my sudden aggression, but I devoured it, my tongue surging into her mouth.

I stepped into her, forcing her to back up toward the mirrors. She still managed to maintain her gracefulness as I manhandled her, so breathtakingly beautiful that it incited a keen hunger I'd never known before.

I grabbed her slender wrists and pinned them to the mirror above her head. My free hand groped at her breasts, palming them through her leotard. Her nipples were peaked against the tight fabric, her body aroused despite the rough way I was handling her. Or perhaps because of it. My Nora was so perfect for me.

And all mine.

She squirmed against me, her sex rubbing my thigh. I wedged it between her legs, so she could stimulate her clit while I ravaged her mouth and tormented her breasts. My cock was rock hard, pressing into her abs. I had to bury myself inside her wet heat, had to claim her as deeply as possible. I would mark her with my cum, a brand that would tell her exactly who owned her lovely body.

I released her wrists so that I could yank her leotard off, baring her small breasts to my rough caresses. She shimmied it down her legs, breaking contact with my thigh in a wild attempt to remove the barriers between us. She was just as caught up in this madness as I was, craving to connect. The fear and violence had stripped away our civilized veneer, and we came together in a rush of primal need.

She fumbled at my belt, her small hands shaking as she stroked her tongue against mine, the kiss stealing her breath. My head was spinning, too, so I tore my mouth from hers and grabbed her hips, turning her around so that she faced the mirror. Her hands fisted around the barre, and I pulled her hips toward me, so that her lower back arched and her cunt was offered to me.

Her pretty tights were still in the way. I tore at the delicate material, the ripping sound harmonizing with the swelling music that still soared through the dance studio.

I shoved her panties aside and wrapped my free hand around her throat, holding her in place for my use. Before I thrust inside her, our gazes locked in the mirror. Her face was flushed, her hazel eyes wide but slightly glassy with lust. My hand was crimson against her tanned skin, the blood of my enemies smeared over her cheeks where I'd grabbed her jaw during our harsh kiss.

More blood splattered my own cheeks, arterial spray from where I'd slaughtered the men who'd tried to take her from me.

"Mine." The snarled word echoed around us, thundering through the classical music as I drove into her wet heat in one brutal thrust.

She cried out, her willowy body rocking in my grip. I firmed my fingers around her throat, restricting her ability to breathe. She could do nothing to resist me, nothing to deny my claim over her entire being. I controlled her body, her breath. I fucked her mercilessly, her tight channel squeezing me with velvet heat that made pleasure gather at the base of my spine. I gritted my teeth and shoved it back. This wouldn't end so quickly.

She released little whimpers with each of my harsh thrusts, squirming in my ruthless hands. I reached around her and ground my thumb against her clit, keeping a firm hold on her neck as I rubbed her in a rhythm that I'd learned she liked best.

She shattered on a scream, the ecstatic sound holding an edge of pain as I forced the orgasm from her helpless body. Her inner walls contracted around me, squeezing my dick and triggering my own release. I tipped back my head and released an animal roar, spilling my cum deep inside her, marking her.

My wife. My Nora.

"Mine."

CHAPTER 11
NORA

"Nora!" My sister's arms closed around me, and the fear that'd plagued me since Luca had left my side melted away.

"I've missed you," I confessed, allowing some of my vulnerability to spill out now that I was safely with Giana. I would be strong for her—I didn't want her to worry about me—but I couldn't help returning her hug with a fierce embrace.

She stepped back so that she could study my face. "How are you, really? I can't believe Father wouldn't let me come to your reception. I've been dying to see you."

I squeezed her hands in both of mine. "Me too." At least Luca had provided me with my own phone, so I'd been able to talk to Giana every day since I'd been forced into this marriage. Still, nothing compared to being in her presence, to see that she was safe and whole.

Giana's chocolate brown eyes were wide on mine. "I heard Luca talking to Father before he left. Did Dante really send men after you yesterday? Are you hurt at all?"

I tensed. I hadn't intended to tell my sister about the kidnapping attempt that'd taken place in our own home. It was why Luca had brought me here, to my father's house. While my husband was out consolidating power and reaffirming alliances against Dante, he wanted me to be somewhere nearby but well-guarded. His estate had been breached, so he didn't want to leave me there while he was in the city. My family home was the closest option, and Luca had secured my father's loyalty through our marriage.

"I'm okay," I promised Giana before she could spiral deeper into anxiety. "Luca protected me."

Giana kept one of my hands in hers as she sank down onto the couch in our sitting room, and I settled in beside her. We didn't break contact; I needed to feel her comforting presence as much as she needed to reassure herself that I was safe and whole. My kidnapping by Luca had been traumatic for her, and worry for my wellbeing had been consuming her.

Her fingernails were too short beneath my soothing touch; they were ragged from where she'd been biting them, a nervous habit she'd kicked years ago.

"Giana," I sighed her name, hating that I was the cause of her distress. "I really am okay."

"But that brute kidnapped you. He forced you to marry him. He's a monster, Nora."

I pressed my lips together, considering. Yes, I'd called Luca a monster when he'd first taken me. I'd hated him for ripping away my future and—even worse—for humiliating me with dark pleasure.

I thought of how he'd handled me so roughly in the dance studio yesterday, after he'd killed the men who'd threatened me. My body was still sore from the savage encounter, but my blood heated to think about it. My new husband was fierce and possessive, but he'd protected me. I'd witnessed shocking violence before, but it was the first time someone had held me afterward. He'd bled for me; he'd been grazed by a bullet while fighting our enemies.

He'd saved me from Alberto's sick lust, too.

And when he'd held me after our reception, he'd told me about his mother's tragic death. He'd made himself vulnerable with me, just for a few minutes.

"He says he wants me to be happy," I admitted.

Giana's brows drew together. "He's essentially holding you hostage to ensure Father's support. How can he possibly expect you to be happy when he's using you like a pawn?"

I shook my head. "I think he means it. Not because he truly cares about me," I explained, "but because he doesn't want to live his life in a miserable marriage."

I wasn't foolish enough to think that Luca cared about my happiness in an altruistic sense. But that didn't mean his tenderness and consideration hadn't softened something in me. I didn't want to be miserable either.

"He built a dance studio for me," I said, my heart lifting at the memory. I'd been so nervous when he'd blindfolded me, but he'd made the entire experience thrilling and special.

"Really?" Giana's jaw dropped, and she quickly snapped it closed. "He asked me to send over your dance outfits, but he didn't say anything else. Well, he didn't exactly ask. He commanded me to send them." She frowned. "He's not good enough for you, Nora."

I gave her a wry smile. "You would say that about anyone who wanted to marry me."

Her eyes tightened. "I'm serious. I hate this. You shouldn't be in this position. Dante was supposed to marry *me*. You aren't supposed to be the one who's forced into a marriage with your kidnapper."

I straightened my spine and fixed her with a steady stare. "That was my choice, Giana. I offered myself to Dante, and I declared myself to Luca when he came to claim his enemy's fiancée. It's too late to take it all back. And besides," I reasoned, "Luca doesn't treat me badly. He says Dante is a sadist. You saw what Dante did to Giorgio when Father arranged the engagement. He's erratic and violent. He scares me far more than Luca does. I didn't want to marry either of them, but Luca saved me from that fate. And he's determined to protect me from Dante now."

No one had ever protected me before, not even my own mother when she'd been alive. She'd loved me, but she hadn't said a word when my father ordered his men to dole out punishments; she'd been utterly devoted to my father and believed that it was his right to discipline his children as he saw fit.

I met Giana's gaze squarely. "I think Luca might be a good match for me," I admitted, hearing the truth in the words. I wasn't simply placating my sister with a pretty lie. "He seems to genuinely like my company, and I believe him when he says he wants to make me happy. I can't ask for more than that."

And he wrung more pleasure from my body than I'd known was possible. My cheeks heated, and I pushed away thoughts of his powerful hands pinning me down, utterly dominating me as he forced me to experience dark ecstasy.

Giana didn't have to know about that part of my marriage. Despite my secret enjoyment of what he did to me, it was still shameful.

There were worse things than a lifetime of pleasure and safety. Luca offered me both. In fact, he insisted upon it. He was relentless in his seduction, and he'd killed to protect me.

"You deserve to be loved," Giana declared.

I shook my head. "That's not realistic, and you know it. I'm trying to make the best of my situation. I don't have to be miserable forever, and Luca has been good to me. I'm choosing to give him a chance."

My sister let out a low hum, thinking it over. "Building you a dance studio is thoughtful and romantic."

I shook my head with a rueful smile. "There's nothing romantic about my relationship with Luca." In fact, I was certain that the studio was a manipulation to persuade me to be less thorny with him. But that didn't mean it wasn't a kind gesture and a grand one at that. "But I think he'll treat me well. We can build a happy home together."

Our children would be safe and loved, and Luca would provide for us. In my world, I couldn't dare to hope for anything more than that.

"I'm sorry to hear that, little bird."

I jolted at Dante's deep, mocking voice, and I was on my feet before he fully stepped into the room. I positioned myself between the monster and my sister, shielding her with my body on instinct.

My stomach dropped to the floor when I took him in, his beautiful features twisted with arrogant amusement. Father was behind him, ushering him into the sitting room. I knew he didn't love me, but his betrayal was a dagger in my heart.

"How could you?" I demanded, voice shaking with rage. My fists clenched at my sides, violence tensing my muscles.

Father's eyes narrowed. "Watch your tone, Elenora."

Giana was on her feet, her fingers digging into my forearm as she tried to edge her body around mine. "Stay away from my sister!" Her demand was high and thin, but she tried to come to my defense as Dante prowled toward us.

I kept my eyes on the monster, but I addressed my father. "You pledged your loyalty to Luca. No one will respect you if you betray him now."

"I was never loyal to that little shit," he seethed, lines of spite drawing deep around his mouth. "He humiliated me. He thought he could back me into a corner and force me to obey him. But Tommaso is dead now, and I won't allow Luca to take control, only so he can push me out of power."

Power. That's all my father had ever cared about. It certainly mattered to him more than his own daughter.

Dante came to a stop before me, barely an inch

beyond my personal space. He towered over me, and I lifted my chin to clash my defiant gaze with his. Vibrant green eyes glittered with amusement, taking in every nuance of my expression as though he was savoring the sight. He held out his hand, an elegant gesture, like a gentleman offering assistance.

"Come with me, Nora." The command lilted with mockery, needling my pride. He already knew my response, and he would relish conquering me.

But there was only one reply I could give him. I would not simply walk out of here with my husband's mortal enemy. Dante would use me to get to Luca. And he might hurt me for his own entertainment in the meantime.

I straightened my shoulders and pushed Giana farther behind me. "I'm not going anywhere with you."

His sharp grin was dazzling, and my stomach flipped with terror. "I thought you might be more difficult this time."

He moved faster than I could comprehend. He'd strolled toward me with such slow, casual confidence that I wasn't remotely prepared when he struck. His long fingers ensnared my wrist, and he pulled me toward him. Before I could claw at his eyes with my free hand, he twisted my arm behind my back and applied upward pressure. My shoulder screamed in protest, and I dropped to my knees with a ragged cry to alleviate the ache. Something sharp pricked the side of my neck, and warmth oozed into my bloodstream.

Giana's horror-stricken face wavered above me. "Leave her alone!"

"No one harms Giana, either." Dante's voice seemed farther away now, but the cold command in his tone still chilled my insides.

I tried to push to my feet, but my limbs were so heavy, and he hadn't let up the immobilizing pressure on my arm. It didn't cause me any pain as long as I didn't struggle. Dante wasn't truly hurting me, but he had me pinned down on my knees.

"Luca will kill you for this." My warning was slow and slurred, my tongue too thick in my mouth.

Drugged. Dante had injected me with something insidious. I couldn't even try to fight him off when he shifted his hold on me. He lifted me up in his arms, and I floated on a warm cloud.

"No," Dante responded smoothly, his voice a low rumble through the haze that blanketed my mind. "Luca won't kill me. But I welcome him to try."

There was no way I'd be able to fight off the man who held me so easily against his powerful body. Stubborn to the core, I tried anyway. I thrashed in his arms, but my limbs barely twitched. My eyelids were so heavy, and I couldn't gather my thoughts to rail at him properly.

"Go to sleep now, little bird. When you wake up, we'll be home."

Home. He wasn't talking about my father's house or the estate where I'd spent my first week of married life with Luca. Dante was taking me home with him, where I would be completely at his mercy. He would lock me in a cage and use me to lure Luca to him.

Fear followed me down into darkness, lingering long after my eyes drifted closed against my will.

CHAPTER 12
DANTE

I looked down at my lovely prize, content to wait for her to wake up. She'd slept the whole journey to my fortified estate in Upstate New York, so she should come around soon. Then, I could fully revel in my triumph over Luca, the bastard.

My revenge was so close that I ached for it, a sharp pang in the pit of my stomach. I'd waited fifteen years for this, and with her help, I'd finally make Luca pay.

The fact that Nora Ricci would be the key to his undoing only sweetened my vengeance. I'd watched the delicate beauty for years, craving her when I knew that her father would never allow me to have her. Thanks to the black mark on my bloodline, he wouldn't have accepted me into his family. Until his fear of Luca forced his hand, and he chose to trust in me.

Now, she was mine, completely in my power.

She looked so fragile when she was sleeping, innocent and serene.

A copper tang coated my tongue, and I swallowed down the sour moment. Luca had taken her innocence, not me. He would scream for that.

But he'd only had her in his bed for a week, and I was certain that noble Luca Vitale wouldn't have corrupted his pretty bride so quickly. Not in the ways I would defile her, and she would learn to love suffering for me.

She stirred with a groan, and a sharp, anticipatory grin stretched my lips. I sat up straighter on the edge of the bed, watching as her long lashes fluttered. Her hazel eyes were glassy at first, her brow furrowed. She was still disoriented from the drugs.

I saw the moment that my face came into focus for her; her eyes flew wide on a gasp, and she scrambled away from me.

"Hello, little bird," I crooned, relishing the tremor that raced over her willowy body. "Welcome home."

She looked around wildly, taking in our bedroom: the rich shades of blue edged with bronze gilding. She was sprawled on our massive bed, her back pressed against the imposing mahogany headboard.

She took in three deep breaths, forcing the air into her lungs. Then she turned a fierce, defiant glare on me. "This isn't my home. Let me go."

The imperious tilt of her delicate chin was delicious. I grinned at her, and she barely wavered at my disconcerting expression. Men had pissed themselves when I turned this cruelly pleased smile on them.

I'd chosen well with Nora. I'd always wanted her, but I'd been prepared to marry her sister when her father approached me with the proposed alliance. But when Nora had defended Giana and defied Giuseppe, I'd known that I couldn't accept another. Giana was shy and timid. Nora possessed a quiet strength and fierce will. I needed a spirited woman who could handle the darker things I wanted to do to her without breaking completely. I had no desire to be married to an empty, mindless shell of a woman.

"You're not going anywhere," I informed her.

"This is your home now, with me. Luca took you from me, but he'll live to regret that."

She swallowed hard, but she kept her defiant posture and stared me down. "My husband will kill you if you touch me."

I reached for her, and she flinched. I touched her face without hesitation, tracing the line of her cheekbone before running my thumb over her lush lips. The brazen way I handled her with such intimacy made her tremble, and the sight went straight to my head: a high that was my drug of choice.

"No, he won't kill me," I informed her. "And he's not your husband anymore. I am."

She blinked, jaw dropping for a moment. "You're insane."

"No, my dear. I'm not. We're getting married. You were always meant to be mine, and we're sealing our union today." I took my hand from her face and gestured to her right, where I'd laid out the white gown that I'd chosen for her. "Time to get dressed."

She froze, wide eyes fixed on the dress, as though it was a snake that might strike at her if she made a sudden movement. "I'm already married to Luca."

"Luca won't be a problem soon," I assured her. "We'll make it legal once I've removed him as a threat. But the ceremony is happening now. I won't wait to have you as my bride. I won't let him take one more thing from me."

She fisted her shaking hands at her sides and set her jaw with defiance. "If you want to rape me, you don't have to humiliate me first."

Anger tightened my gut. "Is that what Luca has taught you to expect? Did he rape you on your wedding night?"

The bastard might be noble, but he was entitled. I hadn't expected him to abuse Nora, but I wasn't all that surprised that he would take what he wanted from her as her husband.

She paled. "My wedding night with Luca is none of your business."

I scowled, and she edged back an inch. "So, he did force himself on you. Don't worry, little bird. I'll make him pay for that too."

"It wasn't like that," she insisted. "And you won't make him pay for anything. He killed those two men you sent after us. He risked his life to save me. He won't stop until he gets to me, and he'll make sure you scream before you die."

"Then what was it like?" I ignored her threats.

She was right: Luca would come for her, and I would be ready. He wouldn't win. "What did your dear *husband* do to you on your wedding night? Was he your white knight then?"

She pressed her lush lips together, her eyes sparking with hatred. She loathed me for making her face the truth. Luca might've killed to protect her, but he'd also violated her.

I leaned in closer, letting her see the stark truth in my eyes. "You will beg for my cock before I give you what you really want."

I would enjoy every second of her slow surrender, until the day she finally welcomed me into her gorgeous body. There were so many wicked things I could do to her in the meantime, such fun ways to toy with her and torment her until she knelt at my feet and begged me to fuck her.

She shook her head, features slack with horror. "Never," she hissed.

I let out a low chuckle, thrilled at her defiant spirit. "We're going to have a lot of fun together, pet." I brushed a quick kiss over her chilled cheek and pulled away. "Now, get dressed. It's past time to make you my wife."

She glanced from me to the wedding dress and

back again, as though she didn't dare take her eyes off the threat I posed.

"Go on," I prompted, crossing my arms over my chest. "Put on your wedding dress."

I anticipated further delicious defiance, but she shuddered and shifted away from me, reaching for the gown with shaking hands.

I frowned, not ready for our game to end just yet. "Am I truly so terrifying, little bird? I didn't think you were so weak."

Her eyes flashed, and she rounded on me.

Good.

"It's not weakness. It's self-preservation. You're a sadist. I saw what you're capable of. I don't intend to give you a reason to strangle me too."

Irritation pricked my spine. "You mean what I did to that motherfucker who hit you? He was lucky that I needed to make a deal with your father. It's the only reason I spared him. I should've cut off his hand instead."

The color drained from her face, and my annoyance flared. My bride should be grateful for my protection. She'd seemed pleased with the fact that Luca had killed for her.

I rolled my shoulders, shrugging it off. Her

devotion would grow with time. I'd waited years to claim what I truly wanted: power, revenge. I could be patient with my wife. Nora would be mine in every way, and she would give herself to me eagerly soon enough.

She scooted away from me and got to her feet on the opposite side of the bed, making it a barrier between us. Her shoulders straightened, and her gaze clashed with mine once again.

"Are you going to watch me change, you sick bastard?"

I clicked my tongue at her. "Watch your language. You're right: I am a sadist. You'd do well to remember that."

I waited until she reluctantly reached for the gown before I turned my back to her, indulging her desire for modesty. Eventually, she'd surrender herself to me fully, and her body would be mine to admire and play with whenever I pleased. I was content to toy with my bride for a while longer.

CHAPTER 13
NORA

The nightmare was happening all over again, but it was so much worse this time. It'd been awful enough when Luca had kidnapped me and forced me into marriage. This time, a madman held my hands in his as the officiant droned his way through the wedding ceremony. We stood in a cavernous dining room, a space large enough to host several dozen guests, but not as large as the ballroom where I'd married Luca. Despite the vastness of the room—empty save for a handful of witnesses, the officiant, Dante, and me—the ivory walls seemed to press in on me, the gilding on the intricate crown molding glittering at the edges of my wavering vision.

I blinked away the sheen of tears and slipped further behind my composed mask, trying to hide from Dante. His vibrant green eyes were keen on mine, attempting to slice straight to my soul. Despite his beauty, there was something innately disturbing about the terrifying capo with a fearsome reputation. He watched me with a stomach-churning mixture of amusement and hunger, his sharp features alight with triumph.

I was nothing more than an object to him, both a pretty trophy and vulnerable bait. This sham wedding signified his victory over Luca, and I was meant to be the key to my husband's undoing.

I had no doubt in my mind that Luca would come for me. Not because I'd deluded myself that he had deep feelings for me, but because his pride and authority wouldn't survive the shame of another man stealing his wife.

I can make you happy. Let me. The memory of his strange command made my eyes burn. Because even if there was no love between us, I'd softened toward my domineering husband. I'd started to dare to imagine a future of comfort and safety with him.

Now, Luca's life was on the line because of my father's treachery. Dante didn't seem at all concerned at the prospect of my husband coming to take me back from him. He was ready for an assault, and he intended to make Luca suffer before he killed him.

This insane ceremony was meant to seal Luca's fate: Dante thought he could marry me because my real husband would be dead soon.

"Do you, Elenora Ricci Vitale, take Dante Torrio to be your husband? Do you promise to obey him, honor him, and keep him for better or worse, for richer or poorer, and in sickness and health, and be faithful to him so long as you both shall live?"

The vows issued by the officiant were nearly identical to the ones I'd made on the day I'd married Luca. *Honor* and *obey*, in particular, stuck in my mind. These sick men expected me to be a dutiful wife, an accessory to their lives without a will of my own. Even Luca had demanded my unquestioning obedience, humiliating me with dark pleasure when I didn't immediately comply.

I swallowed the bile that rose at the back of my throat, shoving the poisonous thoughts about Luca away. He was my only hope of salvation, and guilt nipped at me for even thinking of him in the same way as sadistic Dante.

"It's your turn, darling," Dante crooned. "Say *I do*."

My lips were numb, but somehow they formed the words: "I do."

I had to say the lie. I didn't have a choice. Dante would hurt me if I didn't comply.

I am a sadist. You'd do well to remember that.

I kept my face serene, not allowing my features to so much as twitch with the disgust and dread that boiled inside me. I stared at a spot directly between Dante's dark brows, allowing his fierce grin and dancing eyes to blur into the periphery.

When it came time to exchange rings, he grasped my hand tighter and slid Luca's wedding and engagement rings off. Smirking, he dropped them to the floor like garbage. The soft, musical sound of precious metal pinging on wood lanced my heart like a blade.

I tried to yank my hand away from his rings, but he held me fast. He'd chosen a diamond eternity band and an enormous cushion cut emerald surrounded by diamonds for an engagement ring. The gemstones glittered, so bright that my eyes stung.

I took a deep breath and tore my gaze away from the rings that might as well have been shackles.

It doesn't mean anything, I told myself. *We're not really married.*

Luca was still my husband, not this monster who was looking at me like I was a decadent treat he couldn't wait to devour.

The officiant declared us married, completing the farce of a ceremony. "You may kiss the bride."

I tensed, my beatific smile slipping. I tried to pull my composed mask back in place, but fear shuddered through me in a shockwave, cracking it.

Dante cocked his head at me, his gaze bright with amusement as he watched me crumble ever so slightly. He studied me as though I was the most fascinating thing he'd ever seen, his full, intense attention fixed on every nuance of my expression.

I straightened my spine, defiance sparking through my terror. His dark amusement chafed at my pride, provoking me to betray a glimmer of the fire that raged deep in my chest. I was furious at him for doing this to me, and I was angry at my own powerlessness to physically resist cruel men like Dante.

All I could do was endure, but I was sick of meekly surrendering my body to heartless monsters who only wanted to use me for their own nefarious ends.

Dante's eyes searched mine, and a delighted smile illuminated his angelic features, making him almost painfully beautiful. The effect was both stunning and terrifying.

"No," he said slowly. "I don't think my bride is ready for a kiss. Not yet."

I lifted my chin. "I will never be ready to kiss you. Luca will kill you slowly if you touch me."

He chuckled and shook his head. "Already so loyal to strong, handsome Luca?" he mocked. "Even after he raped you on your wedding night?"

"He didn't rape me," I seethed. It hadn't been like that.

Had it?

I shoved away the treacherous thought before it could fully form. Luca had always ensured that I felt pleasure. He'd never hurt me.

"Let's see just how badly you want to get back to your beloved." Again, that lilting, mocking tone.

I bristled. Luca wasn't my *beloved*, and Dante knew it. He was enjoying twisting my words, trying to goad me into snapping completely.

Before I could swallow my indignation and claw back the composure that would protect me from his cruelty, his hands bracketed my waist. The world spun, and my abdomen collided with his shoulder. Instinctively, I struggled, beating my fists against his lower back as he carried me off, just like Luca had done when he'd stolen me away from Dante on our wedding day.

He palmed my bottom through the layers of organza that made up the skirt of my white gown, brazenly groping me. I thrashed and cursed him, and the bastard laughed.

Chilly air kissed the bare skin on my arms, and everything swirled around me as Dante put me back on my feet. He grabbed my hips and turned me away from him before wrapping a corded arm around my waist, tugging my back against his hard chest.

His big body practically enfolded mine, and I shuddered at his raw power. He wasn't quite as broad as Luca, but he had a couple inches of height on my husband. His muscular frame was more than strong enough to completely overpower me.

A cold breeze raced over my arms, teasing through his body heat that surrounded me. We were outside a huge mansion built of stone that made it appear more like a castle. A circular drive surrounded a massive fountain, and the sound of splashing water was incongruously tranquil in comparison to the abject terror that fluttered in my chest. A forest stretched out before us, the only gap in the trees allowing for the winding driveway. It disappeared into the shadows, the twilight making the leaf-strewn grounds darker than the illuminated front porch, where Dante held me fast.

"You want to get back to Luca?" Dante murmured, his voice a heated caress on my neck. He released my waist, and cold washed over me. "Run."

All my muscles locked up tight. I knew he was toying with me. It would be impossible for me to run away in this voluminous dress and high heels. If I tried to take the path, he would be able to follow easily. But if I took to the trees, I was likely to get lost in the wilderness. I had no idea how large this estate was or how it was fortified. Even if I managed to reach the edges of his property, it was likely heavily guarded, especially considering the fact that he was bracing for Luca to attack.

"Don't you want to fly away, little bird?" Dante cooed. "Here's your chance."

I rounded on him, tipping my chin back so that

I could meet his sparkling eyes. "Stop toying with me."

He grinned and traced the line of my clenched jaw. "I haven't even begun toying with you, pet. But if you're ready to beg me to fuck you, I'll take you back inside." He clicked his tongue at me. "I didn't think you'd give in so quickly. You must like me more than I thought."

I recoiled from his familiar caress. "I hate you," I spat. "Don't touch me."

"You don't want me to touch you? Then you'd better run fast, darling. Feel free to take off the dress and heels if that makes it easier for you. I'll even give you a five-minute head start."

I stood stiffly, forcing my back to remain rigidly straight when instinct warned me to drop my eyes. Suddenly, his hand wrapped around my throat, squeezing. I tried jerk away, but his other arm banded across my lower back, trapping me against his hard body. His eyes flared with sick pleasure when I gasped for air and found none. My lungs seized, and I thrashed against him. He kept my arms pinned at my sides, tucking me closer to him like a lover. My heart hammered in my constricted throat, all my instincts for flight igniting as I twisted in his firm grasp.

He leaned into me, until his shockingly green eyes filled my wavering world. His full lips brushed mine as he commanded, "Fly, little bird."

He released me abruptly, and I stumbled back, gasping for air. My lungs burned, and the trees swam before me. I took a stumbling step away from the monster, desperate to escape. His low laugh drew a shudder to the surface of my skin, and I lurched toward the woods.

"Four minutes and fifty-two seconds," he prompted. "You'll have to move faster than that, pet."

A growl caught in my abused throat, and I kicked off the high heels that hobbled me. My fists sank into the organza skirt that hampered my movement, hiking up the material until it cascaded around my upper thighs. I didn't have time for embarrassment to stall my flight for so much as another thundering heartbeat; I had to get away from Dante.

My feet pounded against the cold asphalt as I raced down the driveway, sticking to the smoother track for as long as possible. I'd have to veer off into the trees soon, but I would spare my tender soles for the first few minutes to put distance between myself and my insane captor. Taking to the woods would be my only option if I wanted to hide from him, but I had no idea how to get off the grounds if I strayed too far from the drive.

His laughter faded beneath the whoosh of my own panting breaths as I sprinted away from him. When the drive curved to the left, hiding me from his view, I sped right, breaking into the tree line. Slick leaves cushioned my bare feet, a small mercy that protected me from rocks that might pierce my skin.

"Nora!" Dante thundered my name from the direction of the path, and I pressed deeper into the woods, away from him. He'd started to pursue me. I would have to evade him amongst the trees and pray that I could find my way off his property somehow.

Something grasped my skirt, yanking me to a stop. I shrieked, terror spiking through me at the prospect that Dante had caught me. I stumbled and fell, the organza ripping as I tumbled into the leaves. I clamped my mouth shut, cursing myself for my scream.

"Nora." This time, his voice was melodic, amused at my folly. He was getting closer.

I grasped my skirt and wrenched it free from the tangle of thorns that'd caught it. Some of the gossamer material remained strewn over the grasping vines, but I didn't have time to cover my tracks; I'd already given away my location when I'd cried out, and Dante was too close.

I clambered to my feet and started running again, forced to move more slowly as the trees grew thicker. More brambles clung to the traitorous skirt, leaving a shredded white trail for him to follow. For an insane moment, I considered ripping off the dress and running naked through the woods.

But the fear beating at the base of my skull wouldn't allow me to stop long enough to strip. My feet kept moving, altering direction every time he called out my name, trying to keep as much distance between us as possible.

I burst into a small clearing, and damp grass sprung beneath my feet, such a different sensation than the slick leaves that'd slipped and slid beneath me as I'd tried to run through the woods. A large wooden shed dominated the center of the grassy space; this must be where the groundskeepers kept their equipment.

My heart sank. I probably wasn't very far from the house if I'd stumbled upon this place. I had no concept of how long Dante had been chasing me, but night had fallen, and the full moon illuminated the clearing.

He called my name again, and my blood ran cold. No, Dante hadn't been chasing me. He'd been herding me.

He'd let me run myself to exhaustion, but he'd simply edged me back toward the mansion as he made me aware of his pursuit; each time he'd called out for me, I'd run in the opposite direction.

I cursed myself for a fool and raced behind the back of the shed, tucking my bright white dress behind it just as Dante entered the clearing. He didn't say a word, but I heard his even footfalls pound the earth as he neared the shed. His singsong whistle pierced the air, shooting toward me like an arrow to shred a hole through my lungs. I couldn't breathe. He was so close...

The door to the shed slid open. My heart leapt. He was going inside to look for me. He must've expected me to hide in the dry, relatively warm space.

I darted across the clearing, back toward the dark woods. My white dress was a beacon in the moonlight, and desperation to hide in the shadows clawed at my insides. If I could only evade him, I might stand a chance of saving myself. Escaping this estate was unlikely, but I could hide until Luca got here. I knew he would come for me, and if Dante didn't have me as a hostage, Luca would be able to attack him at full force. I wouldn't be the reason my husband was murdered. I wouldn't be the reason that Dante killed him and took everything that was rightfully his. I wouldn't let him—

Strong arms closed around me, tackling me to the ground mere feet from the edge of the woods. His low laugh clashed with my scream, and panic spiked through my heart.

Something looped around my right wrist, and rough fibers scratched my skin as it drew taut. Before I had a moment to register what was happening, Dante pulled my arm close to my chest, grabbing my other forearm so he could pin it against my opposite shoulder. Moving with the swiftness of a striking snake, he tugged on the rope that ensnared my right wrist, whipping it around my body so that both of my arms were bound tightly against my breasts. I shrieked and thrashed, but my legs kicked out at nothing. He was behind me, his powerful arms caging me as he wound more rope around my torso, thoroughly trapping my arms so that my hands were useless to fight him off.

My stomach sank, even as I thrashed. He hadn't gone into the shed to look for me; he'd gone in to retrieve the rope that now cruelly immobilized me, rendering me helpless to resist him. He'd pushed me to this clearing by design. He'd planned this sick scene from the moment he'd told me to run.

I threw back my head and howled out my fury. The bastard kissed my cheek and released a happy hum that rolled over my skin in a toxic wave. He was enjoying my terror, my impotent rage.

I writhed, somehow managing to contort my body so that I fell onto my side. I twisted my hips and kicked at his angelic face, wanting nothing more than to break his nose and make him bleed.

He easily snagged my ankle and wrapped more rope around my calf, weaving it in a tight, diamond pattern faster than my fear-addled brain could follow. My free leg whipped toward him, and he pressed his weight against me to pin my knee to my bound chest, trapping my foot between our bodies. He continued his swift work on my other leg, lashing rope around my thigh and drawing it tight enough to edge my panic with pain.

When three of my limbs were effectively immobilized, he slowed his progress, savoring my struggles as he bound my free leg. His eyes were bright with delight, his lush lips drawn in a feral grin, as though the chase had unleashed something primal and predatory in his soul. Any civilized veneer he'd ever possessed had slid away, leaving nothing but the maddened beast that was Dante Torrio: the truth at his core.

He fisted the ropes around my torso and dragged me upright, forcing me onto my knees. The bindings around my calves and thighs shifted, the taut rope digging into my flesh with bruising force. A ragged cry tore from my chest, and I tossed my head: the only part of my body I was capable of moving freely.

My ruined white dress pooled in the grass around me, making me gleam like a virgin sacrifice under the full moon.

Calloused fingertips trailed along my throat, making my nerves jump and dance beneath the gentle caress. It was shockingly tender in contrast to the painful bindings that held me fast. My screams choked off into something like a humiliating whimper, and my entire body vibrated with terror.

"Poor little bird," he crooned. "Don't you like having your wings clipped? You didn't really want to fly away, remember?"

A curse was on the tip of my tongue, but it came out as little more than a garbled plea as my teeth chattered. I was so cold down to my bones. I shuddered in the ropes, fear gripping my psyche like sharp black claws.

"Don't be afraid, pet," he soothed, caressing my chilled cheek. "You'll learn to love being caged."

"Please..." I managed to force out the single, desperate word, but he shushed me gently, like I truly was nothing more than a spooked animal.

Fear had reduced me to a primal state, and he'd ripped away my ability for fight or flight. I was thoroughly trapped and powerless, snared by Dante. He was even more terrible than I'd allowed myself to imagine, just as sadistic as Luca had claimed.

Luca. I longed for my husband, for him to save me like he had when Dante had sent men to our home to threaten us. I wanted Luca to make Dante bleed and scream for what he was doing to me.

But Luca wasn't here. I was utterly alone with the beautiful madman who seemed to want nothing more than to unravel me completely, to reduce me to a fear-ridden, sobbing mess.

He reached around me as though to gather me up in an embrace, and he tugged at the knot that held the binding firm on my chest. As the coils of rope loosened, he pressed down on my shoulder, forcing me lower on my knees. The diamond patterned bindings on my legs bit deeper into my flesh, a throbbing ache that made me cry out.

The pain distracted me, ensnaring my attention as Dante swiftly unwound the rope from my torso. For a few clumsy, desperate seconds, my arms were free. All my poise and composure had been ripped away long ago, and my wild attempts to fight him were fumbling and laughably uncoordinated.

He dodged my flying fist and grabbed my wrists, drawing both arms behind my back and securing them there with a lashing of rope. To my horror, he gripped the bodice of my strapless gown and yanked it downward, baring my breasts to the chilly air. My body was on fire as the cold breeze rippled over the surface of my skin. Icy fear still encased my bones, but somehow, my flesh was burning in contrast to the frigid air.

Rather than ravaging me, Dante returned his attention to the rope. I was thoroughly immobilized, but he tied me tighter, moving at a leisurely pace now that I had no hope of hitting out at him. Pain was a dull throb on my bound legs, digging deep with every pulse of blood through the length of my limbs.

My captor wound the rope around my bare chest, the abrasive fibers lightly scratching my sensitive skin. My nerves sparkled beneath it, tingling with awareness as he kept my body on high alert. The binding framed my breasts, drawing tight until they were thrust out on lewd display. His eyes darkened as he continued his perverted work, amusing himself with tightening the bindings to the edge of pain, until my breasts swelled and became hypersensitive to every brush of his calloused fingertips.

"You're sick," I accused on a ragged whisper, my breath coming in shallow gasps.

"And you're even more beautiful than I imagined," he replied, completely unperturbed by my insult.

He trailed the abrasive rope over my tight

nipples, and sparks ignited on my skin, dancing down my abdomen in hot lines. They pinged along my clit, lighting up my sex with carnal awareness.

My cheeks burned.

No. Not again. Luca had forced me to feel pleasure in order to ease his harsh claim over my body, but surely, I wouldn't be capable of enjoying any aspect of what Dante was doing to me.

He caught my peaked nipples between two lengths of rope and pulled it taut at my back, pinching the sensitive buds. My head dropped back on a wail, a sound of desire and despair.

"So beautiful," he rumbled, nuzzling my hair.

A small, broken sound keened from my chest, and I felt his cruel smile against my neck as he trailed his hot tongue along my vulnerable artery. He kept my nipples trapped as his free hand skimmed up my bound and aching thigh. More sparks danced along my soft skin as he traced around the diamond patterns that dug into my tender flesh, as though he was memorizing the shape of them through touch.

"Please," I whimpered when his fingertips brushed the edge of my underwear. I couldn't bear this. My soul wouldn't survive the shame of what was to come if he continued toying with me.

"I want my kiss, my pretty bride," he murmured, brushing his lips along my collarbone.

"I'll do it," I panted, trying to squirm away. All I earned were deeper bruises on my bound legs. "I'll kiss you. Just let me go. Please..."

He shushed me again, and I squeezed my eyes shut, as though I could block out the horror and humiliation of what he was doing to me. He gave the rope around my chest a firm tug, pinching my nipples at the same time as he pressed his thumb against my clit. Even through my underwear, the pleasure point tingled and pulsed.

"Come for me, Nora." His deep voice caressed my name, far more intimate than his mocking endearments. He'd stripped my soul bare, and he stared straight into me, those green eyes practically glowing in the moonlight as he compelled bliss from my unwilling body.

Tears streamed down my face as the pleasure built at my core, coiling my muscles tight beneath the cruel bindings. A soft cry hitched in my throat, and ecstasy crested.

"That's it," he encouraged, caressing me with merciless intent. "Let go. Give yourself to me."

I gritted my teeth and tried to shove the pleasure back. I didn't want to give myself to this monster. I didn't want to give him anything, certainly not my pride, which he was wrenching away with every assured, rhythmic stroke over my clit.

"Ah-ah," he chided, the rope pinching my nipples with searing, abrasive heat. "Don't fight me, little bird."

He pressed down on my pulsing clit, forcing pleasure to flood my body. My head tipped back on a primal scream: a shriek of rage and release.

His lips sealed mine, his mouth crashing against me as he devoured the sound of my pained ecstasy. His tongue lashed deep, ravaging me as he took full ownership of my entire being. He ripped away my modesty, my dignity, my freedom; he stole my very breath as he kept me locked in his cruel kiss, wringing more dark pleasure from my body as I writhed and jerked in his ropes.

My release peaked, but he didn't release me from the brutal kiss. He continued to ravage my mouth as I was reduced to a quivering mess, all the strength draining from me as the pleasure trailed off. I could do nothing against him. Shame blanketed me with suffocating heat as his tongue tamed mine, and I allowed myself to drift.

"You did so well, Nora." His praise skimmed

over me, drawing a shiver to the surface of my skin.

I wanted nothing more than to melt into the chilly grass and pretend I didn't even exist. So when he gently lowered my body to the cold ground, I didn't squirm or struggle. I simply laid there and stared up at the stars, counting them until the numbers in my head became meaningless.

He was slowly freeing me from the rope, dragging it along my sensitized skin as he loosened the knots and uncoiled it from around my stiff limbs. I hissed in a pained breath when blood rushed back to the braided furrows the bindings had left in my flesh. He made soft, soothing noises and murmured more words of encouragement. I tuned it all out, studying the moon. Everything turned surreal, my body pulsing with aching pain and residual pleasure as my mind floated.

Dante loomed over me, his towering body blocking out the moon as he stripped off his white collared shirt that he'd worn for our wedding. He shrugged out of it, revealing powerful muscles that rippled in the moonlight. He was so much stronger than me. I'd been a fool to think I could fight him in even the smallest way. He'd cracked my composed mask and goaded out my defiance, only so he could shatter my will more thoroughly than any man had ever managed. A slap to the face would've been a mercy compared to what he'd just done to me.

The beautiful monster dropped to his knees beside me and tenderly wrapped the shirt around me, covering my naked breasts. He trailed his fingers through my hair before caressing my cheek. I felt a slight rasp beneath his thumb, and I registered that my face was dirty.

My entire body felt filthy, and not from the soil beneath us. I didn't think I'd ever feel clean again. Dante had reached deep inside me and left a toxic smear on my heart.

When he lifted me up in his arms, I didn't try to fight. He'd thoroughly subdued me, and I couldn't face further horrors or humiliation.

"Let's get you cleaned up and tucked into bed, pet," he murmured, his tone warm and reassuring. "Don't worry. If you break, I'll put you back together again. You're my wife. I'll take care of you, Nora."

I shuddered and closed my eyes, swallowing against the nausea that turned my stomach. Luca had promised to take care of me, too, but he wasn't here to save me.

I was utterly alone, completely at the mercy of the most monstrous man I'd ever encountered. Luca would come for me, but I wasn't sure how much of my soul would be intact by the time he came to my rescue.

CHAPTER 14
NORA

I pushed the scrambled eggs around my plate, trying to pretend Dante wasn't sitting across the table from me. It was easier now that he'd finished his own breakfast and retreated behind his newspaper. My composed mask was nearly perfect, only the slightest tension around my mouth straining the serene smile. It'd taken more willpower than I'd known I possessed, but I'd managed to hold myself together for nearly an hour so far this morning, ever since I'd awakened to find myself in his bed, caged in his confining embrace.

I'd nearly railed at Dante when he'd shown me the scraps of lace that he expected me to wear for him: lingerie and silken robes that were so scandalous I would feel less exposed if I were completely naked. The garments were clearly expensive but unbearably lewd. He was dressing me up like a sex doll, his little toy.

Or worse, his *pet*. He'd called me that several times last night, especially when he'd bathed me, washing the dirt from my skin. I'd been too numb with shock and revulsion to respond in any way. True to his word, he hadn't forced himself on me or seen to his own physical pleasure.

Although the sick delight in his eyes was far more disturbing than simple lustful release.

I dared to peek up at him through lowered lashes and huffed the tiniest sigh of relief to see only the open newspaper facing me, completely obscuring his cruelly beautiful features. I straightened my posture and cut my sausage into even smaller pieces, making the food look like I'd picked at it.

As I took calming, steady breaths, I sank deeper into my poise and composure, letting it settle over me like protective armor. If Dante wanted a pretty doll, I would give him one. He wouldn't break me down again. If he tried to play with me, I would simply refuse to rise to his bait.

He couldn't eviscerate me if I didn't give him access to my true self.

"You're not eating." The newspaper rustled and dropped away. His vibrant eyes skewered me, spearing straight through my elegant mask.

I blinked and forced my lips to remain pleasantly curved, my gaze soft and demure. "I'm not very hungry this morning."

His brows drew together, forbidding. "I don't care if you're not hungry. You will eat."

Indignation sparked, and unease stirred in my gut. I struggled to remain nonchalant and speared the smallest scrap of scrambled eggs onto my fork. I expected him to go back to his paper, but his attention remained fixed on me as I consumed the tiny morsel. It felt like rubber between my teeth, and I almost gagged as I choked it down.

My fingers trembled with rage, so I tightened my hold on my fork. I couldn't let him see how much this tense power play was riling me. If I looked docile, he would go back to ignoring me. He would stop monitoring my food intake.

"Nora." My name was a condemnation. "I expect you to eat every bite, or there will be consequences."

All my muscles tensed, and I spoke before I

could lock the words behind smiling lips. "I'm not hungry," I snapped.

It wasn't true. My stomach ached with hunger, but the pain of it centered me. It was my choice, my body. This was one of my most familiar and reliable mechanisms for control, and he wanted to rip it away from me.

His movements were deceptively casual as he flipped his newspaper closed and folded it, rolling it up into a tight tube in his fist. His knuckles stood out sharply, the veins on the back of his hand visible. So much power in that single fist, a clear threat despite his calm demeanor.

Gracefully, he got to his feet and strolled around the dining table, keeping me fixed in his incisive emerald stare. My soft smile melted away, but I managed to maintain my stiff posture in my seat.

He stopped when he edged into my personal space, looming over me. His head cocked to the side, a single dark brow raised. "I'll give you one chance to be honest with me." His voice was impossibly deep and forbidding. I suppressed a shiver. "Are you not eating because you're anxious this morning, or is this something you always do?"

My stomach flipped. He knew.

How could he know? No one had ever noticed before, not even Giana.

I swallowed. "I don't know what you mean."

He clicked his tongue at me. "Wrong answer, little bird."

He lashed out, and I tried to dodge the worst of the blow to my face. But it didn't come. Instead of slapping me, his fingers twined in my hair, sinking deep into the heavy locks. He pulled, lighting up my scalp with sparks that edged toward pain. I had no choice but to move where he guided me, forced to shift off my chair and bend over the table beside my full plate.

I thrashed, but his big hand bracketed the back of my skull, pressing my cheek hard against the polished mahogany dining table. Before I could gasp out a protest, he flipped up the hem of my short black lace robe. He'd only given me a scrap of fabric for matching underwear, and cool air kissed my bare skin.

A rush of heat immediately flared on my chilled flesh, accompanied by a sharp *smack*. Stinging pain bloomed where he'd struck me, and I shrieked in impotent rage when I noted the rolled-up newspaper in his fist. Humiliation burned my insides, but he didn't relent. He struck again, ignoring my screams as he hit my bottom with searing swats. The sting morphed into a deep throb, driving the heated pain deeper with each repeated smack. My bottom was on fire, and something terrible thrummed between my legs, echoing the thudding hits.

I squeezed my eyes shut and tried to breathe through the awful sensations, my screams dissipating as I struggled for control.

He pushed his hips against my ass, pinning me against the edge of the table. The wood pressed into my clit, and it pulsed madly at the harsh stimulation through the barely-there panties. I felt his erection, but he made no move to free his cock and drive into my vulnerable body. Keeping me trapped in place, he tugged at my hair to forcibly lift my cheek from the table.

"Look at me," he commanded.

My eyes were wide and a bit wild when they met his, fear thrilling through my system to make my fingers tremble. I pressed them tighter against the table, as though that would be enough to hide my terror from him.

"I know what you're doing," he said calmly, as though we were having a normal conversation over breakfast. As though he wasn't completely devastating me, body and mind. "You're trying to take back some control by not eating. How long have you been doing this?"

I pressed my lips together, holding back the admission. How had he seen me so clearly?

He ran the paper down my side, tracing the gentle curve of my hip. "You're thin, little bird. I thought it was because you're a dancer. But there's more to it, isn't there?"

I didn't reply. My mind whirred. How did he even know that I was a dancer? How much did this monster know about me? He seemed to be looking straight into my soul, as though he knew all my secrets already.

His full lips tugged down in a slight frown, his eyes briefly shuttering as he seemed to focus inward. "I watched my mother waste away like this. I'll be damned if I let my wife do the same."

He pushed his hips harder against mine, and I bucked as my clit ground against the table. He let out a low hum and trailed the paper down the length of my spine, sending sparks dancing along it. My body was hypersensitive, fear and pain setting every nerve on edge.

"From now on, I'm going to make sure you

eat," he decreed, delivering a swift swat to my outer thigh.

I cried out and jerked beneath him, further stimulating my pulsing bud against the table. Shame rolled through me in a hot wave, and I closed my eyes as though that would be enough to hide the truth of my arousal from him.

He set the paper down, right in front of my face—a clear warning of what would happen if I struggled or defied him. Keeping his firm hold on my hair, he dipped his free hand between us, testing the wet heat between my legs. My inner thighs were slick with traitorous desire.

I swallowed a sob before it could escape from my chest. I would not break for him. Even after he'd bound me and humiliated me in the woods last night, I hadn't wept. I'd retreated to a quiet place deep inside myself, allowing my mind to go numb rather than allowing him to see me shattered.

What he was doing to me was barbaric, even more sadistic than anything I could've imagined. When Luca had warned me of Dante's cruelty, I'd expected him to revel in beating me. This was so much more perverse and insidious. He attacked my psyche, not content to simply harm my body.

Luca had pushed me hard when he wanted to make me obey him, but he hadn't wanted to break me. My husband had wanted me to be happy. Dante didn't care if I shattered in his cruel hands.

I remembered his dark words as he'd carried me out of the woods. *Don't worry. If you break, I'll put you back together again.*

I shuddered and took a breath, forcing air into my lungs to prevent them from seizing. I would not sob for him. My composed mask had been utterly shredded, but I could at least maintain some of my dignity, my sense of self.

Mercifully, he didn't force pleasure from me. His grip on my body shifted. He released my hair and gently grasped my shoulders, guiding me upright. He sat down in my chair and settled me on his lap, his strong arms caging me on either side.

He picked up a piece of sausage between his fingers and lifted it to my lips.

My cheeks burned, and I turned my face away. How much humiliation could I endure?

"Open up, pet," he cajoled.

I pressed my lips together. He tapped the newspaper, a subtle warning of what would happen if I resisted.

Loathing made my insides squirm, but I reluctantly parted my lips, letting him feed me. The act was mortifying; he was truly treating me like his pet as he fed me from his hand.

After a few bites, he seemed content that I would be docile for this shameful act. His other hand lifted from where it'd rested warningly on the paper to stroke my hair. I shivered as my body tingled, hating my involuntary physical reactions to his touch. The contact was undeniably soothing in the wake of being punished, when all I wanted to feel was hatred and resentment.

He watched me intently as he fed me, his eyes penetrating so much deeper than my blank expression. I lowered my lashes so that he wouldn't be able to see just how badly he was rattling me.

Despite my despair, I didn't shed a single tear. I would not cry for him. I wouldn't give him the satisfaction.

I would not break for Dante Torrio.

CHAPTER 15
DANTE

Satisfaction was a warm buzz in my veins, a slight high from dominating my beautiful wife.

Beautiful, but too thin. I wouldn't allow her to starve herself.

Her cheeks were pink, and her eyes remained downcast as she took the last bite of her breakfast from my hand. She was deeply embarrassed by what I was doing to her, but that only made me enjoy it all the more. Nora was my responsibility now, and I wanted to care for her. If that meant making her shudder and blush, even better. The darkest parts of me craved this from her, and I wouldn't deny myself. I didn't feel a shred of remorse or hesitation; she was mine, and I could do as I pleased.

We were well matched. I could feel the warmth of her wet cunt on my thigh, making my pants damp where she sat on my lap. I wondered if she still tingled with arousal as I fed her or if it was residual lust from being punished. She'd been turned on by my discipline. I relished the prospect that humiliation also incited her carnal desire.

I brushed a kiss over her pink cheek. "Well done, pet."

She stiffened in my arms, chafing at the praise. She probably interpreted it as mockery, but I was truly pleased with her. I did enjoy toying with her, but I wanted her to be healthy. It mattered to me that she ate a full meal. I wouldn't watch my wife waste away.

I touched my fingers beneath her chin and lifted her face to mine, locking her in my earnest gaze. This wasn't a game. Not this time. Her well-being was too important.

"I'm going to take care of you, Nora," I vowed. "I'm your husband."

Her lush lips pulled back from her white teeth in a small snarl of contempt. "You're not my husband. Luca is. You're just a monster intent on torturing me."

Something hot and possessive swelled in my chest. Luca had stolen my bride, and not simply by kidnapping her and forcing her into marriage. He'd somehow acquired her loyalty, possibly even affection, in the short time he'd held her captive. He'd taken what was mine.

Drawing on years of practice, I kept my expression carefully cool and unperturbed. "You think this is torture, darling?"

She didn't know the first thing about true suffering. I would shelter her from harm. I would protect her from everyone who might hurt her. Except me.

I would never brutalize her, but she would suffer for me. In the woods last night, she'd been breathtaking as she'd screamed in my ropes and begged for mercy.

If it weren't for that bastard Vitale, I would've been the first man to touch her virgin pussy. The orgasm I'd forced from her quivering body would've been her first with a man. I would've been the one to introduce her to sexual pleasure, to own that piece of her soul forever.

Luca would pay dearly for that. I had plans for

him, once he arrived to try to take Nora back from me. He would fail, and I would bring him lower than he ever could've imagined. Death was too merciful for my most hated enemy.

She didn't answer me, and her eyes sparked with spite.

I hadn't broken her to my will. I had no desire to crush her spirit completely, but she would learn to obey me. I needed her to be more malleable by the time Luca arrived, or she would spoil my plans for him. He would come for her soon. I had no doubt that he was currently gathering the men and firepower necessary to launch an assault on my fortified estate. He might be here in mere hours.

I needed to accelerate her obedience training.

I guided her off my lap, setting her on her feet before taking her hand in mine. "Come on, little bird. Time to show you around your new home."

She hissed in a sharp breath, and I watched as she caught her lower lip between her teeth, holding in a retort. My wife was no longer calmly composed, but she was still resisting me, tempering her responses to maintain some small sense of control.

But she had no control, not in this house. Not

with me. It was time she understood that. I would imprint the lesson deep in her psyche, so she would know that I owned her, body and soul.

I led her out of the dining room, and she followed with light, graceful steps. She truly did have a dancer's form. I'd have to ensure that she had a space to practice. I intended to spoil my pretty wife, as long as she remained compliant and submissive.

As long as she knew that she belonged to me.

Not Luca, the bastard.

I dispelled the sour thought and reminded myself that my revenge was imminent. His attachment to Nora would only make him that much more vulnerable. If he shared the glimmer of affection that she seemed to harbor for him, I would be able to wound his heart while I shattered his pride. I would break him in every way imaginable, and Nora would help me do it.

My wife would serve me well.

As we made our way through the massive house, I acted like her gracious host, showing her the two sitting rooms, games room, study, whiskey lounge, indoor pool, and sauna. The only room where she dared to take her eyes off me and glance around was the library, as though she couldn't help herself. I didn't bother to suppress a knowing smirk.

Her old man had told me her hobbies when I'd asked—dance, piano, and reading. I'd already searched her bedroom at her father's house, and once I gave her free reign of the library, she'd find her own copies of her favorite books tucked onto a shelf I'd reserved just for her.

I decided to save the music room for later, when I'd show her the piano where she could play for just for me. That would have to wait.

We had many years ahead for me to enjoy her musical talents. Luca might arrive any minute now. It was past time to drop the pretense and take her to our actual destination.

I led her to the end of the long hallway and opened the door to the darkened room. I ushered her into the darkness, ensuring that she was in front of me. With one arm wrapped around her waist, I tucked her tightly against my front, trapping her while I turned on the light.

She tensed as soon as the low golden lights illuminated the ominous space. Her head whipped around, something between a wild inspection of her surroundings and an instinctive refusal to accept where she was.

I splayed my hand over her abs, feeling her muscles jump and dance as she squirmed in my restraining hold.

"Let me go." Her demand was breathless, hitching slightly as fear flooded her senses.

I nuzzled her hair and inhaled her soft, floral scent, imprinting the memory in my brain. She was scared this first time, so deliciously frightened and powerless in my arms. My naïve young bride had no idea of the pleasure I would wring from her in this room, when I toyed with her for hours at my leisure. She would cry in pain and ecstasy, and I would savor her tears.

I surveyed the room as she trembled against me, looking at it through her eyes. The massive bed would be familiar enough to her, save for the numerous restraint points on the black metal frame. The large domed cage was obvious, too, but I doubted she'd ever seen the rest of the bondage furniture that waited for her helpless body to be strapped down for wicked torment. Would she even conceive of how I'd bend her over the spanking bench or how I'd cuff her to the St. Andrew's Cross?

If she didn't understand their particular function, it would be easy enough for her to interpret my intentions based on the wall of impact implements to our right. A varied selection of single tail whips, floggers, canes, and more cruel toys of my own design were hung in an artful pattern, each one waiting to lash her with a particular flavor of pain.

"Please..." She squirmed against me. "Don't hurt me."

"Oh, you will suffer for me, little bird. You'll sing for me." I'd never heard a more beautiful sound than her scream of despair and ecstasy when I'd compelled her to come in my ropes. I would force it from her again and again, a lovely song just for me.

Keeping her pinned with one arm banded around her, I reached for the second drawer on the tall black cabinet to my left. She jerked when I slid it open, the soft sound magnified by her fear.

"What are you doing?" she demanded shakily.

I didn't respond. I simply picked up the thick metal cuffs by the chain that attached them and swiftly grabbed her right wrist. The polished stainless-steel cuff clicked into place, shackling her. She cried out in alarm and tried to pull free, but I used the leverage of the short chain to hold her steady while I grabbed her left wrist and secured it with quick precision.

She twisted her entire body, shimmying free from the cage of my arms. I let her go, keeping only the chain hooked around two of my fingers. The simple hold anchored her to me, and she jerked and cursed as I easily led her into the center of the room.

Suddenly, she stopped dragging her feet and launched herself at me, small hands curled into fists. I'd denied her instinct for flight, and now my little pet wanted to fight me. She was so delicate and fragile. She'd hurt herself if I didn't get her fully under control.

I would always take care of my wife.

Keeping the chain in my fist, I lifted her hands above her head, preventing her from punching out at me. With my free hand, I grasped the hook that hung from the ceiling and locked it through the short length of chain, leaving her dangling by her wrists. She kicked out at me, so I stepped away, enjoying the pretty jangle of metal as she struggled.

I crossed to the corner and grasped the opposite end of the chain, which extended from where I had it running through a metal ring directly above her head. I pulled on it slowly, watching as her flailing movements became gradually restricted, her body drawing taut until she was forced to stand on her toes.

A wicked image of her wearing pointe shoes in this position flashed across my mind. Yes, I'd keep her in that predicament another day. Soon.

As it was, she couldn't do more than stretch her body to its limit and quiver, waiting for my next move.

"Are you uncomfortable, darling?" I asked, teasing her.

"Fuck you," she seethed.

I laughed, delighted at her fire. Taming her would be a pleasure.

"Not yet," I reminded her. "Not until you beg."

She pressed her lips together, as though sealing the words inside forever.

My low, cruel chuckle rumbled through the room, and she shivered as though it was a physical touch.

She was truly breathtaking, her lithe body barely concealed by the black lace I'd dressed her in. The robe parted slightly between her breasts, and it was short enough that it barely covered her shapely ass in her current stressed position.

"Should I show a little mercy?" I asked, soft and reasonable.

"I doubt you're capable of mercy," she hissed, turning her head to the side as she struggled to spear me with her hazel glare.

I clicked my tongue at her. "So hostile. You don't know me at all, my pretty bride. You have no idea what I'm capable of."

I loosened the tension on the chain by two inches, allowing her feet to stand flat on the black tile floor. When she was in the position I desired, I secured the chain and went to retrieve the next item for her torment.

Her wide, fearful eyes darkened with confusion as I approached with the long metal bar and knelt before her. She tried to kick at my face again, but I released a small, warning growl and grabbed her ankle. Her weight dropped on her bound wrists, and she cried out at the flash of pain. I stared up at her, keeping my firm hold on her ankle as she struggled to find her balance on one foot. Her eyes shot daggers at me, and she bared her teeth like a trapped animal. I brushed a kiss over her calf, communicating my pleasure with her.

She was responding to my games beautifully.

I secured a leather cuff around her trapped ankle, then grabbed the spreader bar. The cuff was attached to one end of the bar, and now that I had her secured, I could move her where I wished. I lowered her bound foot to the tiles, pushing her legs wider apart. The second cuff was around her other ankle within seconds, forcing her to remain open for me. Completely vulnerable to anything I wanted to do to her.

I skimmed my hands up to the backs of her knees, my fingertips teasing into her inner thighs. She whined and writhed, making music with the chains. I stared up at her from where I knelt between her feet, a position of supplication where in reality, I held all the power.

Her lovely eyes glittered, and her chin quivered before she quickly bit her lower lip.

So, my pretty wife didn't want to cry for me.

That wasn't her decision to make. I wanted her tears. I wanted her to come completely undone and cling to me—the only person who could put her back together again once she shattered.

I leaned forward and ghosted a kiss over her clit, feeling the tight bud through the barely-there panties I'd bought for her. She gasped and tried to rock her hips away from me, but she had nowhere to go. Reveling in her helplessness, I tongued her clit, teasing her. A ragged scream tore through the room, a sound of pure frustration and rage.

It went straight to my head, and I laughed as pleasure swept through me. My cock stiffened, but that desire was secondary to my craving for her submission. I could take her body when she was truly mine, once she gave herself to me fully and eagerly. Until then, I would find my own twisted release in tormenting her, dominating her.

"Stop," she groaned, jerking against her bonds but unable to move away from my mouth.

I pressed one final kiss to her cunt and relented. There would be time to make her come later.

"You haven't earned an orgasm yet," I told her, getting to my feet.

Her eyes burned into mine. "I don't want an orgasm, you sick bastard. I want you to let me go."

"I'm not nearly finished with you, pet." I patted her cheek, and she snapped at my fingers as I quickly pulled them out of range.

I grinned. She was delightful.

And she was all mine. This wouldn't end until she admitted that absolute truth.

CHAPTER 16
NORA

A humiliating sound like a whimper escaped my clamped lips when Dante ripped away the lace robe that provided me with a scrap of modesty. He tore the delicate material with swift jerks of his big fists, stripping me with brutal efficiency. When the remnants of the robe fell away, he made quick work of destroying the lewd panties he'd forced me to wear for him.

I wanted to rail at him for being a sick, twisted bastard, but beneath my incandescent ire, I was terrified. Dante was unlike any man I'd ever encountered before. He was tormenting me, but this wasn't a punishment. Not like when he'd bent me over the dining table and swatted me with the newspaper. Not like how Luca had spanked me when he'd first kidnapped me. Not even like when my father's guards had slapped me when I stepped out of line.

Those were all consequences for my actions. Justified or not, there was a clear reason for my suffering in those instances.

I had no frame of reference for whatever game Dante was playing with me now, and that scared me even more viscerally than his pursuit through the woods. I'd thought I had a chance of escaping him then. Now, I was bound and naked, completely at his mercy.

But he had none. I'd been right when I'd said he wasn't capable of it. Looking into his glittering green eyes, all I saw was selfish desire and twisted triumph.

He liked my fear and my pain. This was what Luca had meant when he'd warned me that Dante was a sadist.

Luca. I longed for my husband to come and save me from this monster. It'd been nearly twenty-four hours since Dante had taken me from my father's house. Surely, Luca would come for me soon.

But not soon enough. Not before Dante made me suffer for his pleasure.

Satisfied at my nakedness, he stepped away and crossed the room, approaching the horrific wall of torture implements. He tapped one long finger against his chin, rubbing it over the stubble that darkened his sharp jaw. Even in profile, he was heartbreakingly beautiful, a fallen angel with those high cheekbones and dark curls: the Devil himself.

He cocked his head, then reached for a whip with dozens of long, thick leather falls. I shuddered as he grasped the handle with something like reverence, his elegant fingers trailing over the polished wood. He turned his wrist, testing the weight and balance of the flogger. With a short, satisfied hum, he turned back to me.

Fear gripped my muscles tight, and the chains jangled as I twisted against my restraints. His full lips spread in a slow smile as he approached me, those vibrant eyes sparkling with anticipation.

"Please," I begged, my rage smothered by terror. "You don't have to hurt me."

He touched the whip beneath my chin, lifting my face to his where he towered over my much smaller frame. "Oh, little bird. I know I don't have to. I *want* to hurt you. And you scream so beautifully." He leaned in close, brushing his cheek along mine so that he could whisper in my ear like a lover. "If you just let go and embrace the pain, I'll help you fly."

"I don't want to be in pain," I whispered back, my throat too tight to speak more assertively. "Please, Dante, I—"

"*Master*," he corrected. "I'm your master, pet. Your husband. When we're together like this, you'll address me with the proper respect."

Despite my terror, I bristled. "You're not my husband. Luca is."

He clicked his tongue at me, chiding. "That was a foolish thing to say, darling. You *are* my wife. You will learn to love being mine. Before we're finished here, you'll admit that you belong to me. You'll know that I'm your true master."

"No one is my master," I hissed. "I don't belong to anyone but myself."

I'd said the same thing to Luca on our wedding day, when he'd kidnapped me and forced me into marriage.

I hadn't won against him.

Looking into Dante's beautiful eyes, I feared that my loss this time would be far more devastating. I was naked and chained, completely helpless to prevent him from whipping me. He would do whatever he wanted to me, and there was nothing I could do to stop him.

He shook his head, dark curls tumbling around his perfect face. "I admire your spirit, but you will learn when to yield to me, Nora."

He stepped away, and I sucked in a ragged breath. I released it on a scream when the first strike landed, the leather falls kissing my bottom with a loud *slap*.

He made a low sound of disappointment. "I barely tapped you. You'll take a lot more by the time I'm finished with you."

Terror flooded my mind, seizing control of every inch of my body. I didn't want this. I had to get away.

I twisted and yanked against the restraints. The metal cuffs dug into my wrists with bruising force, and my eyes burned. I blinked rapidly, barely maintaining the willpower to prevent the tears from falling in thick, desperate streams.

The whip touched my spine, just at the base of my skull. The heavy falls dangled down my back, brushing over my hypersensitive skin. A strangled cry of animal fear tore up my throat. More pain than I'd ever known was coming, and he would enjoy inflicting it.

His hand spanned my stomach, stilling my frantic struggles. He traced the line of my spine with the whip, a gentle caress.

"Hush now, pet. Calm. You'll hurt yourself."

"You're the one who's hurting me," I accused through chattering teeth. I stopped yanking against the cuffs, but my entire body shook.

"Yes, and you'll take the pain for me," he replied calmly, as though I was the one being irrational. "But I don't want you to cause yourself harm. You'll damage your wrists if you keep pulling against the chain like that."

He was right; my wrists ached already. If I continued struggling, I'd tear my skin away, possibly even damage the delicate tendons.

I had no hope of fighting him if I couldn't use my hands once I was free. Because even though my brain acknowledged the futility of attacking him, the primal part of me wanted nothing more than to claw his eyes out, to protect myself in whatever way I could.

He continued to stroke me with the whip, petting me with the implement that would torture me. The gentle sensation of the soft leather sliding down my back was completely at odds with the way my body was braced for pain. The dichotomy muddled my mind, sensation and expectation polar opposites.

I tried to breathe, and my lungs seized. A choked, hitching sound caught in my throat: the threat of a harsh sob.

I swallowed it down and gritted my teeth, searching deep inside myself for a shred of defiance. Fear would not break me. Dante could play his sick mind games, but he wouldn't touch the core of who I was. I couldn't allow it. I didn't think my soul would survive it.

He brushed a kiss over my cheek, communicating his satisfaction at my capitulation; I'd stopped struggling.

He moved behind me once again. I had less than a heartbeat to brace when I heard the *whoosh* of the flogger cutting through the air. Then fire raked across my bottom, a harder hit than the first.

I bit my lip, holding in the terrified cry that wanted to escape. Truly, it hadn't hurt more than when he'd struck me with the newspaper. In the moment, the fear that clawed at my brain was far more potent than the slight burn of the whip.

I could master the terror. It would not rule me.

I would survive this. I would endure, like I always did.

"That's better," he approved, noting a change in my posture. "You're very brave, Nora. But you still think you're in control. You aren't. Not with me. Let go."

A harsher lash, a deeper sting. A hundred needles pierced my skin before the pain sank into my flesh in a heavy throb. He took up a steady rhythm, landing twin hits on each side of my bottom to kiss my tender skin with heat. I pressed my lips together and breathed through it, letting the pain wash over me, until it was a low buzz that blanketed my mind.

"You're doing so well, pet." There was no hint of mockery in his praise. Whatever I was doing pleased him.

I stiffened, hating him. He wanted me to accept the pain. I wanted to resist, but how could I do anything else? The only way to resist was to absorb the pain and deny its power over me. I would not cry. I would not beg. I would not—

Fire lashed my upper thigh, and a ragged cry burst from my chest before I could contain it. Another hit. Another involuntary scream.

I'd thought there was pain before, but this was

incandescent, my sensitive skin burning beneath the harsh rake of the whip.

"So beautiful," he sighed over my next shriek.

My bound hands curled to fists, rage fueling my resistance. I clung to my will by a thread. Settling into the pain at the beginning had been a mistake; now that I'd let down my walls against it, more flooded my system like a burst dam.

"You're my wife, Nora," he said with the weight of an absolute truth. "Not Luca's. Tell me you're mine."

Loathing was a white-hot sun at the center of my chest. I would never belong to this monster. I would never willingly give myself to him.

Luca didn't own me either. I belonged to myself. No one was my master.

"I'm not yours," I forced out through gritted teeth.

Rather than becoming incensed, the bastard chuckled. My blood ran cold. He was happy for the excuse to hurt me more.

I had to protect myself. Taking a deep breath, I remembered how I'd floated in the woods last night after he'd utterly humiliated me. I took another breath and retreated to a dark, quiet place deep inside myself. Screams made my throat raw and sore, but the pain didn't decimate me. I let it rip through me, until it was a rushing tide, and I floated on it.

The hits stopped, and his body heat caressed my side. His warm breath fanned my neck, drawing a shiver to the surface of my skin. His calloused palm skimmed down my back, stroking me with a lover's comforting touch.

"Tell me you're mine, Nora," he murmured in my ear, his voice threading into my muddled mind with insidious intent. "Tell me you're my wife."

It didn't matter what I said. I wouldn't mean it. Saying the words didn't make them real.

"I'm your wife, Dante." The lie rasped from my abused throat.

His vibrant eyes filled my world, peering straight into me. He cupped my cheek in his big hand, his fingers threading through my hair. Mindlessly, I leaned into the caress, welcoming the soothing contact after the overload of pain.

"You don't mean that, darling."

My gut twisted. I licked my dry lips. "I do," I lied again, an echo of the false vow he'd forced me to make during our sham wedding.

He frowned and shook his head almost sadly. "Don't lie to your master."

"You're not my master," I shot back before I could think. My mind rejected it on a soul-deep level.

He hummed and studied me for long, agonizing seconds, until I started to squirm with apprehension.

"No," he said slowly. "You don't believe that you're mine. Not yet. But I can be very patient, little bird. For today, I'll settle for unquestioning obedience."

Perverse relief flooded me, making my knees weak. I could obey. It wouldn't mean anything. I'd spent my entire life yielding to cruel men in order to protect myself.

"I'll do whatever you want," I said, a pleading edge to my tone. "Just don't hurt me again."

He massaged my scalp, and I almost groaned at the decadent sensation. "I won't damage you, Nora. But I will have your true submission. This doesn't end until you give in."

His fingers trailed down my neck, tracing the line of my artery. A pleasurable shudder rolled through me, my body welcoming the tender contact. His touch lowered, until he circled my nipples. Callouses rasped over delicate skin, and my breasts grew strangely heavy.

"No," I moaned. "Please..."

The pain was bad enough, but the forced pleasure was worse. I didn't want to enjoy any aspect of what he was doing to me. If he made me come, he'd chip away at another piece of my soul. He'd devastated me when he'd bound me in the woods. Looking into his beautiful face, his sharp features firm with determination, I knew that this time would be worse. He wanted to break me down, to make me malleable.

I could promise to obey him over and over again, but he wouldn't relent until the words were reality.

The whipping had weakened my defenses, as had my acceptance of his tender touches. I'd let myself be swept away by sensation, and now I was vulnerable to the pleasure as well.

He gently pinched my nipples, tugging at the tight buds and lighting up my body with warm sparks. They danced down to my sex, making my clit tingle.

My head dropped back on a despairing groan, and I closed my eyes to try to shut out the nightmare.

He cupped my nape, directing my eyes back to

his steady emerald stare. "Ah-ah, pet," he chided. "Stay here with me."

He tweaked my nipple hard, and my eyes flew wide, locking on his.

"You like pain with your pleasure, don't you, my pretty wife?" He released me from the pinch and stroked the abused peak. I shuddered and sighed. "You're so perfect, Nora."

The praise left me cold. I let it frost my skin, helping me start to go numb.

He slapped my sex, making my clit sting. I cried out and tried to edge away from him, but the restraints held me wide open. He spanked me again, punishing my most vulnerable area. My core contracted, ready to be filled.

"Stop," I begged.

He shushed me and continued, until my clit throbbed in time with the rapid beat of my heart. My eyes stung with shame, and a hot tear scored my cheek. I blinked hard, but another tear fell.

A strangled growl of pure hatred slipped through my bared teeth. He kissed my lower lip and smiled at me, thrilled with my predicament.

He brushed his lips over my wet cheek, tasting my tears. He released a growl of his own, a sound of primal male satisfaction.

He relented spanking me, rubbing my clit in firm circles. All my muscles tensed as I tried to deny the bliss that coursed through me. My inner walls fluttered, and my thighs grew slick with arousal. He forced me higher, spiraling up and up, until my entire body was wound tight.

He withdrew his hand, and I cried out at the loss. I immediately bit my lip, and more mortified tears spilled.

He reached down and picked up the whip where he'd dropped it at my side.

"Don't," I choked out. I didn't want him to hit me again.

Instead of flogging me, he touched the polished wooden handle between my legs, coating it in the wetness on my thighs. My mind blanked, unable to process what I knew was coming.

His thumb returned to my clit, and the hard, slick handle pressed at my entrance.

"Relax," he urged, rubbing my pleasure point and wringing more bliss from me.

Against my will, my body softened. The whip slid in an inch. I clamped down tight, refusing to accept what he was doing to me.

His lips touched mine in a coaxing kiss. I was

too distracted by the unyielding penetration to think about biting him.

"You're mine," he murmured, relentlessly stimulating my clit as the handle slid deeper inside me. "Tell me."

"I'm yours," I lied, squirming to get away. The whip went in another inch. My inner walls contracted around it, and my attempt at resistance further stimulated me.

"Again," he crooned.

"I'm yours." I was panting, sweat mingling with the tears on my cheeks.

"Tell me you're my wife."

"I'm your wife." The whip hit my g-spot, and I released a ragged cry of ecstasy and despair.

He turned the handle, smiling with dark satisfaction as bliss sang through me. "Very good, pet. So obedient."

He didn't care that I didn't mean it. All that mattered to him was my complete devastation.

"Come for me," he commanded, another order that I had no choice but to obey.

He pressed down on my clit and nudged the handle against my g-spot. I shattered on a wail, my head tossing as ecstasy wracked my body. I shuddered and writhed, and he wrapped a strong arm around my waist to steady me, releasing my overly sensitive clit. He left the whip inside me for a minute as aftershocks pinged through my core in little lighting strikes.

All my muscles gave out, my body going limp in the wake of my intense, cruel release. He caught me, reaching above my head to free the cuffs from the chain that held me aloft. He carried me the short distance to the massive bed and laid me out on the mattress. His fingers rubbed over the goosebumps on my arms before he found the catch at the sides of the cuffs, freeing me with a soft click.

As I rubbed my aching wrists, he unbuckled the cuffs around my ankles and pulled the spreader bar away. He sat on the bed beside me, leaning against the headboard. His hands bracketed my waist, and he guided me onto his lap. I felt his erection pressing into my bottom, but he made no move to have sex with me.

He'd fucked me with his whip instead, forcing me to feel pleasure from the cruel implement that'd caused me pain. It was more perverse than anything I ever could've imagined.

My cheeks were hot beneath my tears, shame burning me up inside.

I had no fight left in me when he began to pet me, stroking my hair while he cuddled me close. He kissed my wet cheeks, savoring the taste of my tears.

"It's okay to cry," he said, comforting. "You're so pretty when you do. I'll always take care of you, Nora."

Luca had told me the same thing, but he wasn't here to save me. My longing for my husband was tinged with resentment. I shouldn't have any soft feelings toward him. He'd kidnapped me and forced me into marriage, just like Dante had done.

My heart twisted. I was so tired of being treated like an object, a pawn.

Or worse, Dante's *pet*.

Something vibrated beneath me, and Dante pulled his phone from his pocket.

"What?" The irritation that pinched his features morphed into a maniacal grin. "I'm on my way."

He pressed a quick kiss to my forehead. "I have to go."

My stomach lurched. Luca must've come for me at last. And Dante looked delighted.

He thought he would beat my husband. He was certain of it.

All I could do was pray that he was wrong. Dante was arrogant and cruel; he could've miscalculated.

He lifted me up in his arms, and I tensed when he carried me to the large, domed cage in the corner.

"Please don't put me in there." I didn't like tight spaces.

He shushed me. "You'll be safest in here, little bird."

He placed me in the cage and slammed the bars in my face, securing them with a padlock. My fingers wrapped around the cool metal, as though I could pry it apart.

"Don't leave me in here," I begged.

"Don't worry, darling. I'll be back soon."

He turned and walked out of the awful room, leaving me caged and cold. Ice encased my bones, and I drew my knees up to my chest, hugging them tight.

I didn't want Dante to come back. The only man I wanted to come for me was Luca, my real husband.

CHAPTER 17
LUCA

The bastard had taken my wife. He would suffer before he died.

Fear for her clawed at my insides, digging in deeper than ever. It'd torn me apart for the day that'd passed since her father had betrayed me and given Nora to my enemy.

Giuseppe would pay for that soon. But my first priority was getting her safely away from the sadistic madman. Cold sweat beaded on the back of my neck at the thought of what he might've done to her already, in the time it'd taken me to gather my allies and make our way to his remote estate.

She's not dead, I reminded myself. He wouldn't have killed her. She was a valuable hostage.

As long as she was still breathing, I'd heal her from whatever he'd put her through. In the short time I'd been married to her, I'd developed a soft spot for my pretty, spirited wife. The humiliation of Dante stealing my bride chafed at me, but the fear of failing her was equal to it.

I took a breath and hefted the semiautomatic in my hands, comforted by its weight.

"Brace," the driver warned as he accelerated the armored SUV, heading straight for the gates that guarded Dante's home.

Gunfire ricocheted off the bulletproof car, Torrio's men trying to take us out before we could breach the property. Our SUV was at the head of the convoy: ten armored cars filled with men who were fiercely loyal to me. I'd selected only the ones I trusted most, not daring to risk Nora's safety by relying on someone with questionable loyalties. I was paranoid after Giuseppe's brazen betrayal. I wouldn't repeat the mistake and end up with a bullet in the back of my head.

The SUV punched through the gates with a terrible grating sound, the entire car lurching at the impact. The barrier gave way, and we tore down the drive, past the men who were shooting at us from the guard towers set into the imposing stone wall that surrounded the entire estate.

Dante had been ready for an assault, but he hadn't counted on the resources I had at my disposal. The arrogant bastard probably thought everyone in the organization would turn on me when my father died and he took my wife: a symbolic seizure of my power.

But his arrogance would be his downfall. He would die screaming, and I'd have Nora back, safe in my arms.

Bile burned the back of my throat at the thought of my fragile wife in his cruel hands. I swallowed hard and shoved the dark thought away. I didn't have room in my brain for fear now. All I could do was focus on my goal with violent intent, keeping my senses sharp.

Tires squealed as we pulled up to the house, the back of the SUV skidding around the circular driveway. I burst from the car, along with the men I trusted most in the world. Gabriele and Lorenzo were right behind me, the burly brothers' faces set in identical grim masks.

I kept the car door open as a shield, and—unsurprisingly—more bullets slammed into it. There were guards at the front of the house, firing from the entryway before ducking back inside for cover. I whipped into the open when the bullets stopped flying for a heartbeat, pulling the trigger on my rifle. A dozen sharp reports rent the air, and someone screamed inside the house.

Gabriele bellowed behind me, a sound of rage and panic. I whirled, and something slammed into my shoulder, the bullet testing the efficacy of my tactical vest.

Fuck!

Lorenzo was on the ground, gasping for air. Blood poured from a gash on the side of his neck, where a bullet had torn through the delicate flesh. The pulsing crimson streamed onto Gabriele's hand where he pressed it hard against his brother's ruined skin.

"Get him into the car!" I bellowed, fear for my friends rising up and threatening to choke me.

Behind me, more of my men screamed. The gunfire was coming from a different direction now. I looked up and saw four snipers on the roof.

"Go, go, go!" I shouted, peppering the front door with suppressing fire as I rushed for the house.

I was vaguely aware that some of my men

followed, but many of them were still pinned down by the snipers.

Somehow, I managed to avoid more bullets as I burst into the house, rifle raised. Something sharp slammed into the side of my neck, and I spun to face the threat. There was no one to my right, only an empty corridor. It wavered strangely.

More gunfire directly behind me. More screams.

I whirled and stumbled, the world tilting. The barrel of my gun drifted toward the floor as my fingers began to go numb.

Confusion threaded through my fear, and I swatted at the thing stinging my neck. A silvery dart fell away and clattered onto the hardwoods beneath my boots.

"Fuck." The curse was slurred, and I took a step toward the door, struggling to get back to the cover of the SUV.

It'd been too easy to get to the house. Dante had wanted this.

I remembered what the traitor, Federico, had said when he tried to take Nora and me from our home: *Dante wants her alive. She won't be harmed. He wants to see you both.*

Dante wanted us both alive. He didn't intend to kill me quickly.

My stomach lurched, and I took another stumbling step toward the exit. I would have to regroup and come back for Nora. I was useless to her if I let him capture me.

Through my wavering vision, I saw several of the cars pulling away, retreating. The others remained as ruined husks, dead and bleeding men strewn across the pavement around them.

I'd led them all into a trap. My friends were dead because of me.

No. Because of Dante.

The motherfucker appeared in my line of sight, grinning like a madman. I lunged for him, and my knees gave out. I tried to clench my fists, but my arms were so heavy at my sides.

"Fight me like a man, you coward," I seethed, my tongue too thick in my mouth.

A single black brow raised. "But you're not a man. Not anymore. You're mine."

He leaned against the doorjamb and crossed his arms over his chest, settling in to watch me fall. The last thing I saw before the darkness claimed me was his glittering green eyes, shining with feral triumph.

CHAPTER 18
NORA

My heart dropped to the floor when the door to the dungeon opened, revealing Dante's imposing form. He shot me that maniacally pleased grin as he stepped inside. I choked on a horrified gasp when I saw who was behind him: two men dragged Luca's bulky body between them. His head lolled forward, and his knees skimmed the tiles.

He was naked.

"Luca!" I grabbed the bars on the cage, trying to wrench them apart so I could get to my husband.

He groaned at my sharp cry, and his muscles rippled. He shook his head slightly, but he couldn't seem to lift it.

"What did you do to him?" I demanded of Dante, my voice too high-pitched.

"He's fine, darling. He's just drugged. I don't intend to kill him."

My stomach churned. Judging by Dante's sharp smile, he planned something worse than death for his rival.

The two men heaved Luca's limp body onto the bed and shackled his wrists and ankles to the bedposts. Nausea stirred in my stomach. My strong husband, my savior, was a captive. He was stripped and powerless, just like me.

"Luca." This time, his name left my lips on a broken moan.

Somehow, the nightmare had gotten so much worse. Deep in my heart, I'd expected him to save me. There hadn't been an alternative in my mind; the prospect of remaining trapped with Dante was unbearable.

Luca stirred at the sound of my voice, and Dante slapped him hard across the face.

"My wife wants to talk to you," he sneered.

Luca blinked slowly, eyes glassy as he struggled back to awareness. His powerful limbs twitched, and chains rattled as the cuffs held him fast. He grunted and blinked again, shaking his head slightly as though to throw off the fog of the drugs.

"Please," I begged, turning my attention to Dante. "Let us go. You don't have to hurt him."

His green eyes were pitiless, spearing my heart with an icy blade. "No. I've waited too long for this. It's his fault that you're involved now. If he hadn't stolen you away from me, you would have no part in this. He will suffer for taking what's mine, and you will help me."

I wanted to rail at him that I didn't belong to him, that I never would. He was deranged and unfathomably cruel. He'd demanded my obedience when he'd humiliated me with the whip, but he hadn't broken me. He'd known that I didn't mean it when I said I was his wife.

I didn't dare give voice to my defiance now. Not when Luca was completely vulnerable to Dante's sadistic whims.

Luca came back to full awareness with a roar of pure rage. The chains rattled against the metal bedframe, and his corded muscles bulged as he fought the restraints. His ochre eyes were fixed on me, wide and wild.

I shrank deeper into the cage and covered my breasts, mortified at my nakedness. Dante had brought me low, and Luca was witnessing my humiliation.

"What have you done to her, you sick fuck?" he bellowed at our captor.

Dante simply smirked at him, watching his fruitless struggles with dark amusement.

Luca twisted in his bonds. "Let her go," he snarled. "You have what you want. I'm right here."

"Yes, you are," Dante purred. "And you're not in a position to make demands. You don't understand yet, but Nora does. Shall I show you how obedient my wife is?"

Luca glanced around wildly, searching the room for another woman. I saw the moment he understood what Dante meant.

"She's mine," he growled. "Nora is *my* wife."

"Not anymore," Dante retorted. "We're married, and as of now, you're no longer her husband. You are no one. You are nothing."

As Luca struggled and cursed him, he calmly walked toward me and unlocked the cage. He held out a hand, a pretense of gentlemanly assistance. "Come on out, little bird."

Refusing his mocking help, I crawled out onto the tiles and quickly stood to recover a tiny shred of my dignity. I wouldn't remain kneeling at his feet for one second longer than he forced me to.

Before I could cover my breasts again, he grasped my hips and turned us, so that I was positioned in front of him. My bruised bottom pressed against him, and I felt his cock stiffen. He was getting off on this, the perverted bastard.

Keeping one arm braced around my middle, he lifted his other hand to my breasts, toying with my nipples until they tightened to firm buds. I was still sensitive from the terrible orgasm he'd forced from me with the whip, and I shuddered as my nerves crackled and danced for him.

"Isn't my wife beautiful?" he asked Luca, ignoring my true husband's bellow of rage.

"Stop," I begged, watching red rings form around Luca's wrists where the cuffs cut into his skin. "Please, let us go."

The monster's low, delighted chuckle rumbled through me. "Oh no, pet. You're both mine now."

"Why are you doing this?" I asked, still pleading with him to stop this insanity and see reason. "You want to be the boss? You don't have to torment us to take control."

Suddenly, his hands sank into my hips, and he flipped me around to face him. His emerald eyes sparked with fury, and his beautiful features twisted into a mask of pure hatred.

"I've been waiting years for this revenge. Luca killed my brother. He will pay, and your pretty pleas won't save him."

My mouth went dry at the raw loathing that burned in his fierce gaze. I saw no mercy there. He would make Luca scream. He would break him. And he would somehow involve me in his torture.

"I won't hurt him." My assertion came out as a strained whisper. The insane light in Dante's eyes unnerved me to my core.

His grin cut into my chest, stabbing at my heart. "I don't intend for you to hurt him, pet. You're going to suck his cock."

Horror sucked all the air from my lungs, and for a moment, all I could do was shake my head mutely.

He wanted me to do to Luca what he'd done to me: he intended for me to force Luca to feel pleasure against his will. He wanted to utterly humiliate my strong, domineering husband. Dante would rip away all his control in the most devastating way, and he wanted to use me to do it.

"I won't." I managed to force the refusal

through my constricted throat. "I won't torture him like you tortured me."

"You raped my wife?" Luca roared, blood sliding down his arms from where the cuffs were shredding his wrists.

Dante sneered at him, as though he was something disgusting on the bottom of his shoe. "I haven't fucked *my* wife yet. And I won't until she begs for it. I'm not an animal like you. I can control myself."

No, Dante wasn't an animal. He was the Devil himself. I'd been right when I'd first thought of him as a fallen angel. How could someone so beautiful be so cruel?

The Devil returned his attention to me. "You can do as I say and suck his cock, or I can go back to my original plan of slowly flaying him alive. I can make it last for weeks, possibly longer. He's strong enough to take a lot of pain before his heart gives out."

He placed a hand on the knife hilt at his belt. "It's your choice, darling."

I swallowed against the burn at the back of my throat and peeked at Luca. He'd stopped yanking at the restraints. His big body quivered with the effort of holding still when adrenaline coursed through his system.

I knew the exact, awful sensation he was experiencing. I'd felt it when Dante had caught me and bound me in the woods last night, allowing me to run for my life before snaring me.

His games were perverse and twisted. I didn't want to play, but he wasn't giving me a choice. I couldn't let him hurt Luca.

We would survive this. We would endure.

I straightened my shoulders and ignored the way Dante stroked my spine with satisfaction.

"I'm sorry," I whispered to Luca, stepping toward his bound form.

He looked past me, ochre eyes shooting daggers at his enemy. "I will kill you for this."

"For getting a blowjob from my lovely wife? You should be on your knees, thanking me. Eventually, you will do just that."

Luca bared his teeth at him, but his expression softened as I approached. "It's okay, Nora."

His soothing tone made my eyes burn, and I was too horrified to hold back the tears. Dante had already opened the floodgates when he'd made me come all over the handle of his whip. The tears fell freely now.

I crawled over Luca, kneeling between his spread knees to position myself near his cock. I stared down at it, unsure. We'd never done this before. Luca had always taken my pussy, not my mouth.

Dante's low laugh caressed my nape like a toxic wave. "You haven't claimed her mouth yet, Luca?" He placed a hand between my shoulder blades, urging me forward. I bent at the waist, bracing my arms against the mattress at either side of Luca's hips.

I took a breath and tried to retreat into myself once again, so I could endure what was to come.

"Don't worry, pet," he soothed. "I'll guide you through it. I'll teach you to love sucking cock. You can practice on Luca until you're ready for me."

Luca snarled, and the chains jangled. I looked up at his bleeding arms, my vision wavering through my tears.

"Don't," I begged. He was hurting himself, and this was terrible enough without knowing that he was in pain.

His granite jaw was sharp enough to cut as he gritted his teeth and stilled. His dark eyes pierced my soul, and he gave me a tight nod: permission to continue and a promise not to struggle.

"Take him in your hand, Nora," Dante instructed, so coolly composed while Luca and I were coming apart at the seams. "Stroke him."

I wrapped trembling fingers around Luca's shaft. It jerked and stiffened beneath my hesitant touch.

Dante laughed again, the bastard. "I won't even have to drug you to make you hard. You're even weaker than I thought, Vitale. Although," he continued, stroking my hair, "my bride is stunning enough to tempt any man."

"She's not yours," Luca ground out.

"Nora, darling. Squeeze his balls. Hard."

I jolted. "No!"

Silver flashed in my peripheral vision, and a blade was suddenly pressed to Luca's rippling abs, scraping down the trail of dark hair that led to his cock.

I cupped Luca's balls and squeezed, closing my eyes so I didn't have to look at his expression when he released a strangled shout.

Dante resumed stroking my hair. "You're doing so well, pet."

"I hate you." The spiteful words trembled with tears.

"Lick him." There was a bite to the command

this time, the amusement evaporating from his tone.

I opened my eyes and breathed a sigh of relief to find that Dante had sheathed the knife once again. My compliance had made him relent before he cut Luca. I had no choice but to continue.

Releasing my cruel hold on the most vulnerable part of my real husband, I licked his cock: a desperate apology.

"Slower," Dante growled. "Like you're tasting your favorite candy. Savor it."

I ran my tongue along the underside of Luca's shaft and swirled it around the swollen head. He stiffened in my hand, and something salty painted my lips.

"Stroke him with your hand at the same time."

I allowed my mind to drift, distancing myself from my body. What I was doing didn't matter. My obedience was just a survival mechanism. I was saving Luca from torture.

But even as I thought it, I knew he was suffering in my hands. This lewd act—the complete loss of control—would be tearing my strong, dominant husband apart. The fact that I was also being debased right in front of his eyes would make it that much worse.

"Very good," Dante praised.

I wanted to let the humiliating words breeze past me, but they were accompanied by a brush of his fingers over my clit. A shocked cry burst from my chest at the sudden, intimate contact. Luca's hips jerked at the vibration of my lips on him.

My cheeks flamed, but Dante didn't relent. He circled my clit with his thumb, drawing out my pleasure with expert ease.

"Take him in your mouth," he ordered. "Stroke him while you suck."

My tears fell, and I tasted the salt of them on Luca's shaft as I obeyed. Dante stroked one finger into my tight channel, and I hissed against Luca. I was still sore from the whip handle.

Dante shushed me and continued toying with my clit, easing deeper inside me to find the sensitive spot at my core. He crooked his finger against it, and I whimpered as pleasure pulsed through me. Luca's hips bucked again, his cock pushing deeper into my mouth.

I gagged, and he eased back.

"I'm sorry," he said, ragged. "I'm so fucking sorry, Nora."

Another finger swirled in the wetness on my inner thighs—forced arousal from his masterful, manipulative touch. I tensed and went utterly still when he pressed against my asshole.

"Speak to her again, and I'll penetrate her virgin ass," Dante warned.

Luca's lips pressed together, but his dark eyes promised Dante a slow, painful death.

Our captor rubbed my g-spot, lighting me up with unwilling bliss. "Don't stop, darling. You're doing a wonderful job for your first time. See how hard you're making him?"

Luca snarled, but he didn't dare to say anything else, sparing me from the worst humiliation.

"Take him deeper," Dante prompted me.

I fell into a mindless rhythm, pumping Luca's cock while I sucked him as deep as I could. He hit the back of my throat, and I gagged again.

Dante rubbed my clit. "Breathe. You can take more."

My body softened in his expert hands, and pleasure began to ripple through me, starting at my core to reach my fingers and toes. Luca's cock slid into my throat, and he choked on a harsh shout. His powerful body shook beneath me, trembling with the effort of holding himself back. I knew he wanted to take control, to thrust into me and claim my mouth in the way he desired.

But he had no control, and neither did I. We were Dante's now, his toys to play with for his own sick amusement. My body wasn't my own. And I was robbing Luca of his autonomy too.

Luca growled, and his cock stiffened in my mouth.

"Squeeze his balls again, darling. Don't let him come. You orgasm first. Always."

I obeyed, and Luca's rough cry pierced my heart. At the same time, Dante rubbed my g-spot hard, and his thumb ground against my clit. He wrung ecstasy from my body, forcing it to crash through me in waves.

I screamed around Luca's shaft, and Dante's fingers tangled in my hair. He pushed me down, making me take my real husband deep in my throat while I shattered. Luca roared his agonized pleasure, and he released into my mouth.

"Take it all," Dante growled. "Swallow, pet."

As I complied, he stimulated me mercilessly, so that bliss sang through my veins. Every fiber of my being glowed with carnal ecstasy, even as my soul shrieked in protest.

Luca groaned, and Dante finally pulled me off

his cock, allowing me to draw in a gasping breath. Oxygen flooded my deprived lungs, making me lightheaded. The room spun around me, and when Dante released my sex from his demanding hands, I collapsed on top of Luca.

I crawled up his body, half-blind with tears.

"I'm sorry. I'm so sorry."

I wrapped myself around him, clinging to his strong, bound frame.

He trembled beneath me, but his voice was low and soothing when he replied. "It's okay, kitten. I'm right here. I'm okay. It's not your fault."

I buried my face in the crook of his neck and sobbed.

Dante had finally broken me.

CHAPTER 19
DANTE

Something dark and ugly stirred in my chest as I watched Nora cling to my most hated enemy. She was *mine*. My wife, not his. She might not be ready to accept the truth, but I found that I didn't like seeing her cuddling up to Luca. I could be patient with her, but I wouldn't stand here and allow her to sob in another man's arms.

If Nora was going to cry on anyone, it would be me. I'd earned those tears. Her scream of pleasure had been for me, not him.

My hands closed around her shoulders, and I had to pry her away from Luca. She sobbed and thrashed, fighting me so that she could stay with him.

I pulled her into a tight embrace, trapping her smaller frame in my confining arms.

"Hush now, little bird. We're done here."

I frowned when she cried harder, twisting in my grip.

Maybe using her like this was a mistake. Maybe I should flay Luca, after all.

I looked over at him, and I knew I had no better path open to me. His eyes shined with a murderous glint and something more vulnerable. Nora wasn't the only one reduced to tears, although Luca's seemed to be more from impotent fury than hurt.

A cruel, triumphant grin stretched my lips, and I lifted Nora up in my arms. She covered her face with her hands and cried, so I tucked her closer to my chest, comforting her.

My wife would come to accept my sadistic needs. She would learn to love the dark pleasure I offered her. One day soon, she'd beg me to fuck her in front of Luca, and he would know who her true master was. He would know that I'd claimed his bride, his birthright. I had taken everything from him, but he would pay even more dearly.

He'd murdered my brother. For that, I would shatter his soul.

And I would use Nora to break him.

―

Thank you for reading IN THEIR HANDS! I hope you enjoyed this first installment in Dante, Nora, and Luca's dark romance. Their story continues in
IN THEIR POWER.

Also by Julia Sykes

Their Captive Bride

In Their Hands

In Their Power

In Their Hearts

Mafia Ménage Trilogy

Mafia Captive

The Daddy and The Dom

Theirs to Protect

Theirs Forever

Fallen Mafia Prince Trilogy

Fallen Prince

Stolen Princess

Fractured Kingdom

The Captive Series

Sweet Captivity

Claiming My Sweet Captive

Stealing Beauty

Captive Ever After

Pretty Hostage

Wicked King

Ruthless Savior

Eternally His

The Impossible Series

Impossible

Savior

Rogue

Knight

Mentor

Master

King

A Decadent Christmas (An Impossible Series Christmas Special)

Czar

Crusader

Prey (An Impossible Series Short Story)

Highlander

Decadent Knights (An Impossible Series Short Story)

Centurion

Dex

Hero

Wedding Knight (An Impossible Series Short Story)

Valentines at Dusk (An Impossible Series Short Story)

Nice & Naughty (An Impossible Series Christmas Special)

Dark Lessons

RENEGADE

The Dark Grove Plantation Series

Holden

Brandon

Damien

Printed in Great Britain
by Amazon